Stolen Friend

A Luke Larson Adventure

Al Reich

Printed in the United States of America

Packaged by Pleasant Word, a division of WinePress Publishing, PO Box 428, Enumclaw, WA 98022. The views expressed or implied in this work do not necessarily reflect those of Pleasant Word, a division of WinePress Publishing. Ultimate design, content, and editorial accuracy of this work are the responsibilities of the author.

ISBN 1-57921-561-0
Library of Congress Catalog Card Number: 2002117103

This Book Is Dedicated To My Grandsons:

Justice Samuel Winston Heerema
Alfred Elijah William Heerema

CONTENTS

Chapter  1

I wonder what it's like to be like them, not having to work all the time, having time to relax and do whatever they want? Luke thought aloud as he passed the houses in the new development on his way to the hay field to pick up another load. Luke had been raised on a southern Michigan dairy farm and knew no other life than hard work every day. Luke loved being outdoors and enjoyed the animals, but sometimes he wondered if there might be a better way to live. He had to make that decision soon because he was going to be a junior in high school this fall and there had been talk about him going to college. He didn't know if he wanted to go to college, or even what to study if he did go to college, but people said college was important, so he kept thinking about it.

"Luke, what are you thinking about?" asked Jay, his younger brother. "We just passed the road to the field."

Luke pulled into a driveway, then expertly backed the tractor and wagon to get it headed back in the direction they'd come from, and they were quickly on their way to pick up another load of hay. They would have to work late tonight to get all the hay out of the field because it was supposed to rain later. Luke's dad and Gus, his other brother, were milking the cows and doing the other chores so Luke and Jay could work on getting the hay out of the field.

The boys passed another house on their way to the field. The whole family was sitting by their swimming pool, watching the tractor go by as they sipped beverages through straws. Luke was convinced these people were lazy and not able to do a real day's work, but he envied them deep inside because they had time to relax and enjoy life.

He didn't respect most city folk because the few times his dad had hired kids to help work on the farm they never lasted more than a day, especially if the work involved getting in hay on hot summer days. The chaff from the hay would stick to their sweaty skin and they would start itching; that would be the beginning of the end of their work on the farm. The heat in the field was bad enough, but unloading the hay in the barn was stifling, and most of the help wouldn't last more than two or three loads of hay.

Luke at least felt that this type of work kept him in good shape. He couldn't go out for sports because of the work load at home, but he was very athletic and longed to play football and run track.

The boys arrived at the field, and Luke told Jay to drive slowly while he picked up bales and tossed them on the wagon. Periodically Jay would stop and Luke would climb on the wagon to stack the hay so they could eventually pack on eighty-four bales. While Luke arranged the hay Jay quickly counted the remaining bales. "One more load after this," he said.

Most farmers had equipment to make big bales of hay to be picked up by the tractor and transported to the farm but Luke's dad, Al Larson, felt they couldn't afford any new equipment right now.

The boys finished loading the wagon as the sun was beginning its descent, casting long shadows around the load. When they got home, Gus was just coming out of the barn, signifying the chores were done. Luke pulled the wagon beside a long elevator that would carry the bales into the hay mow, located above the barn's milking parlor.

"Mom said supper will be ready in twenty minutes," Gus said as he approached the other boys. "Dad says we should put this load in the barn before supper." Luke and Jay headed for the hay mow. Gus turned on the elevator and started heaving bales on it. The bales were immediately transported upward and disappeared through a window in the barn. Inside, Luke and Jay stacked them in neat rows. Luke would often carry two bales at once to keep up with the endless flow from the elevator. Although Jay was only twelve, he was already a good worker and quite strong for his age.

Eventually the elevator stopped, signifying the end of that load. Luke and Jay quickly went down the ladder and out of the barn door. They were both drenched in sweat, and their faces, necks, and arms were covered with hay chaff so fine that it looked like a green scum. "We'd better wash up," Luke said. "Supper's ready."

Brushing the hay chaff from their shirts and pants, the boys went into the milk house, where there were facilities to wash up. Soon they stepped into the house, which was a typical farm house. They entered through the mud room, a small room where they kept their chore clothes and rubber boots. As they opened the door to the kitchen the smells of supper greeted them instantly and the boys suddenly realized how hungry they were.

"What's for supper, Mom?" Jay asked.

"Roast beef and mashed potatoes," Nancy, their oldest sister answered.

"And corn on the cob," added little Sandra.

Their mother, Martha, turned to greet the boys. She always had a smile on her face, even though she had the job of caring for a family with five children. Soon everybody had gathered around the table. They sat down and held hands as Al said grace. As soon as he said "Amen" the silence was broken and everyone started talking, mostly about the day's events. Soon they had their plates full and it was again quiet as they focused on the good meal before them. "Farmers may not be rich, but they generally don't go hungry," Al often said after a meal.

Tonight Al finally broke the silence. "The Rices lost another dog last night," he said with only passing concern. "Stan Rice told me he was a good watch dog and his biggest, meanest dog. He doesn't know why he would just disappear." It did seem strange to Luke that some neighbors' dogs were missing. He thought of their own family pets, Brownie and Sam. Brownie was a terrier cross of about forty pounds with excellent speed when it came to killing rats around the barn and granery. Sam was a powerful, dark brown dog of unknown origin and weighed about ninety pounds. Luke was especially close to Sam because he had raised him from a pup. He was just a little over three years old now and just getting out of the puppy stage that it seems to take some dogs forever to reach.

Luke's thoughts were interrupted by Jay, who asked if a bear could have taken the Rices' dog. Instantly the boys started laughing but the girls' eyes got a little bigger at the mere thought of a bear in the area.

"There hasn't been a bear seen in these parts for twenty years," Al said. "Likely it wandered off and somebody shot it, although Stan said it never left the property."

Soon supper was finished. The girls started to clear the table. "We'd better get that last load of hay out of the field," Al said. "We can park the loaded wagon in the barn and unload it tomorrow. Jay, you stay home. Gus will drive and I'll stack the hay. Luke can hand the bales to me."

The three were about to leave when out of the barn came Sam. He obviously wanted to come along, now that it was the cool of the evening. When Al started the tractor the two boys sat on the wagon and encouraged Sam to jump up with them, but to the surprise of no one he wouldn't come close to the wagon. Al started down the driveway and Sam broke into an easy lope that would cover lots of ground in effortless fashion. The tractor could go almost twenty miles per hour and Sam maintained that steady run for the three miles to the hay field.

Before long they had the remaining bales loaded and dusk was settling over the land. Al let Gus drive home.

"Better put the lights on," he said and Gus automatically pulled out the switch. The ride back was uneventful and Sam kept his steady pace all the way home, running beside the tractor. Getting down from the wagon Luke met Sam, who wanted attention and did not seem tired in the least. Luke played with him briefly, wrestling and playing tug of war with an old burlap sack.

It was getting dark and the mosquitoes were coming out. Al and the two boys went inside. No pets were allowed in the house and Sam wouldn't even like it in the house, except that he could be closer to Luke. But he knew his place and he had a job, patrolling the yard to make sure all was well at all times. Brownie had been a good watch dog in his day but he was getting older and a little hard of hearing. He spent most nights in the upstairs of the barn on a soft bed of hay or straw, leaving most of the work to Sam, which was the way it should be.

Chapter 2

"Saturday morning," Luke thought as his dad woke him and the other boys to help with chores. The sun was just beginning to rise and it looked like a beautiful day. The ground was moist from an overnight shower. Al, Gus, and Jay went to do the milking, and Luke started his chores, which included feeding the pigs and getting grain and silage for the cows. Luke was exceptionally happy today because he was going on a date with Sue Foster, a girl he had secretly liked for a long time and finally got the courage to ask out. Luke had got his driver's license a few months ago and was going to pick Sue up at seven o'clock with the family car. They were going to a movie and then over to Caruso's, the local teen hangout.

After chores the boys went inside for a quick breakfast. Al had to go to town and the boys had to unload the last wagon of hay. The last bale was just falling off the elevator when the boys' friend, Larry, showed up. Larry lived a quarter mile north of the farm in a small house with his mom and dad. His dad was a truck driver and was gone a lot. Larry always had a lot of free time and would sometimes come over to see the brothers. He was also sixteen but went to a different school than Luke.

"Well, tonight's the big night, right, Luke?" Larry said, his dark brown eyes flashing mischievously.

"Are you gonna kiss her?" Gus asked. All the boys laughed, including Luke, who didn't mind being teased. Indeed, he wondered if he might kiss Sue tonight. He hoped so, because it would be the first time he'd actually kissed a girl.

"Let's go down to the creek," Larry said. "Okay, but first let me tell Mom," Luke replied. Gus and Jay didn't want to take a walk. They'd rather play around the house. Luke and Larry started for the creek but only got a short distance before Sam caught up. Sam loved to go exploring with Luke, especially down by the creek. The creek ran between Larry's house and Luke's place and the boys decided to follow it upstream. Sam was busy exploring but always stayed close to Luke. The creek took a sudden turn and as the boys rounded the bend they could see a muskrat on the bank about forty feet away. Sam saw the muskrat at the same time and charged ahead to catch it. The muskrat's reflexes were faster than Sam's and it quickly dove into the water and safety. Sam spent the next ten minutes trying to find it, sniffing along the banks on both sides of the creek, wading back and forth. Luke finally yelled at Sam and he reluctantly left the muskrat to follow the boys.

Further upstream the boys jumped some ducks, mallards, Luke thought. He carefully guided Sam away in case there were any baby ducks around that couldn't fly. Soon they came to a special place along the creek for Larry. Earlier in the spring he had caught a four-pound brown trout in the hole just below where the boys now stood. Sam was behind the boys as they gazed down into the water. Presently, Luke could make out the form of a trout at the tail-end of the pool.

Chapter 2

"There's one you didn't catch, Larry," he said. Larry saw the trout also and decided it wasn't as big as the one he caught, but made a note to come back soon and try for this one.

"I've got to get back home," Luke said. "It's time for lunch. Then we have to grind feed for the pigs and cows."

"Where are you taking Sue?" Larry inquired.

"To a movie and then to Caruso's," Luke replied.

"When do you have to be home?"

"By eleven," Luke said. "Sue has to be home by then too, so I guess it'll work out."

The boys walked across the fields, climbing over the fences as they came to them. Sam couldn't jump the five-foot-high woven wire fences but he knew how to get over them. He would run along beside the fence, then jump on a fallen tree and leap over the fence and be on his way, chasing after the boys.

When the boys got home, Martha, asked Larry to stay for lunch. Larry said he couldn't, and the boys hastily made plans for the next day before Larry left.

The rest of the afternoon went by too slow as far as Luke was concerned. He had to help his dad work on the John Deere before chores. Finally he was able to go inside and get ready for his date. As everyone sat down for supper all the children talked about was Luke taking the family car and going on a date, with a *girl!* After supper Martha gave Luke some instructions and some tips on driving. Finally Al, in a kidding way, told her to leave Luke alone. Both parents trusted Luke.

Al tossed the keys to Luke, and Luke went out the door. The whole family was at the front door watching him drive down the driveway. He honked and then turned onto the gravel road. At last he had time by himself to think. He was getting more nervous as the time approached to meet Sue's parents. Sue lived in town, about seven miles from his home. He parked in front of the big, two-story white house with green trim and cautiously approached the front door. He took a deep breath and rang the door bell. Instantly the door opened. Sue's younger brother looked up at Luke and then announced to the whole house that Sue's boyfriend was here. Luke's face flushed a little and soon Mrs. Foster came to the door.

"Please come in," she said in a soothing voice that put Luke at ease. She had a pleasant smile and quickly introduced Luke to Sue's father, a rather tall, thin man with graying hair.

"How are you, Luke?" he asked. "Sue has told us a little about you. Do you play any sports?"

"No sir," Luke said apologetically. "I have to help with the farm work and it's hard to get a ride home after practice, so I'm just not able to go out for sports."

"That's too bad," Mr. Foster said.

Presently Sue came downstairs with a shy smile on her face. She was very pretty. Her brown hair was slightly curled and it glistened in the light. She was very popular in school and it had taken all Luke's courage to ask her out. Like him, she had just turned sixteen and had not been allowed to go out on unchaperoned dates until now. Sue was involved in a lot of school activities because she was popular but she also lived very close to school. Luke was well liked in school but not as popular because he couldn't go out for sports. His peers knew he was a good athlete, mostly because of physical education classes and the periodic fitness tests that were given by the gym teacher, Mr. Frye, who was also the basketball and track coach. Mr. Frye had encouraged Luke to try out for track, but track season coincided with spring planting season. Also, most of the farm's sows farrowed in the spring and the new broods of piglets meant more work.

After what seemed like an eternity, Susan told her parents they had to go, and Luke followed her out the front door.

"Nice to meet you," he told the Fosters. Luke opened the car door for Sue and hastily walked around to his side.

Chapter 2

"What movie are we going to see?" Sue asked. They had to drive to Three Rivers to the theater, which had two movies running. Luke had been cautioned to stay away from action-adventure movies with girls so he had decided they would see a comedy with animals called *Snow Dogs*. He knew Sue loved animals and it was a logical choice. Luke occasionally glanced across the car to look at Sue, who was sitting midway between him and the passenger door.

"You look very pretty, Sue," he finally said. Sue blushed slightly and thanked him but then started to talk about school and their common friends and her plans for the summer. Luke loved to listen to Sue talk. He occasionally added a sentence here and there, but she carried most of the conversation.

Soon they arrived at the theater. Luke chose seats toward the back, but not so far back that either of them would feel uncomfortable. Now, should he put his arm around her? He decided to wait and see how things went.

"Do you want some popcorn and soda?" Luke asked. He went to the lobby and got a big box of buttered popcorn and two cokes. He was actually relieved to be by himself for a short time. He realized he must relax and enjoy himself. He'd thought about this time so much that he had become anxious and he was robbing himself of a good time in the company of a beautiful girl. He went back to his seat determined to enjoy the time he had with Sue.

Sue smiled up at Luke as he approached, thanking him for the popcorn. Luke held the popcorn between them and they both nibbled at it throughout the movie. They laughed together and commented about the movie and enjoyed themselves. As the movie ended Luke realized he hadn't put his arm around Sue like he had planned. Did she expect it? He was beginning to doubt if she had had a good time.

"Let's go to Caruso's," Sue said with that warm smile that made Luke feel good.

There was no parking lot at Caruso's so cars parked on the street. It looked busy as they slowly drove by, looking for a parking space. Soon they were walking up the steps to the teen hangout. Luke opened the door for Sue and was instantly greeted with the sounds of the juke box mingled with the voices of a hundred young people all talking at once. He quickly looked around the room, searching for friends.

"Luke! Luke!" came a voice from a far corner of the room. Luke saw an arm waving. It was one of his classmates, Ralph Clime. Sue and Luke started walking in that direction, acknowledging friends along the way. Sue even stopped to talk to Janet, a classmate and fellow cheer leader, for a brief moment, before continuing to Ralph's booth. When they arrived Sue slid into the booth and Luke followed, all the while talking about their lives in the two weeks since school ended. Ralph was with Jennie, which was no surprise. They had been going together for two years already. Sue and Jennie were quickly involved in conversation, so Luke and Ralph continued to discuss the beginning of summer vacation.

"Did you know that Ed Burgess is back home?" Ralph asked. Ed was a year ahead of Ralph and Luke in school. The story was he had quit school, lied about his age, and joined the Marines. Ed was a nice guy who didn't mind talking to underclassmen. Luke had been in gym class with him before he dropped out. Luke knew that Ed didn't get along with his dad and was unhappy at home, but Ed never went into more detail.

"Have you seen him?" Luke asked.

"Yeah he's over there," Ralph said, pointing across the room. Luke saw Ed, who was in uniform, talking to some former class mates. Several kids were standing around him, eagerly listening.

When the crowd around Ed began to disperse, Luke decided to go and say, Hi. He carefully approached Ed and put his hand on his shoulder. Ed quickly turned, looked up, and smiled at Luke.

Chapter 2

"How are you doing?" Ed asked.

"It's good to see you, man." Luke said. "You left so quick I never got to say good-bye."

"I finally made up my mind to leave home and felt the Marines would be a good place to be," Ed said proudly.

"Are they treating you right?"

"They treat me like everybody else, which I guess is fair," Ed said. "I'm through basic training and I'm stationed down south right now."

"Was basic training hard?" Luke remembered all the stories he'd heard.

"Yeah, it was, especially at first, but it was still better than what I had at home," Ed said without emotion.

Doug Jones, a friend of Ed's, interrupted just then. "Did you have to do any Marine push-ups?"

"We had to do some," Ed replied. Luke had never heard of a Marine push-up.

"I bet you can't do ten Marine push-ups," Doug challenged. Ed turned to continue his conversation with Luke, ignoring Doug, but Doug interrupted again.

"I'll give you five bucks if you can do ten Marine push-ups."

Ed looked at Doug for a moment. "Put your five dollars on the table." Ed rose from his chair, removing his coat. Luke noticed that Ed had packed on muscle since he'd seen him last and was confident he would win the bet. Doug, already acting a little nervous that Ed had accepted the challenge, informed Ed they had to be good push-ups with no cheating.

After a few people backed up to give him room, Ed got down on the floor, placing his hands on the floor in front of him so that his thumbs and index fingers touched each other, forming a triangle. He assumed the push-up position and quickly lowered his body until his nose touched the floor in the middle of the triangle between his hands. Quickly his arms brought him up until the elbows locked. Someone shouted "One" and Ed started his second push-up. It was obvious from about the third push-up that he was going to win the five dollars, but he passed ten and just kept going. He finally stopped at thirty, quickly got up, smiled at Doug, put the five dollars in his pocket and didn't look at all tired. Everyone was surprised at how easily Ed had done those push-ups, especially guys who had attempted that kind of push-up before. Luke had never heard of a Marine push-up, but he could see that it would require a lot of shoulder and tricep strength.

Several people were congregating around Ed so Luke went back to the table where Sue and Jennie were. Ralph had left the table to see what was going on and came back just after Luke.

"What happened?" Jennie asked. Ralph explained and the girls listened politely but quickly went back to their conversation when Ralph finished. Ralph then turned to Luke.

"I don't think I can do one Marine push-up. Can you?"

"I never even heard of a Marine push-up before tonight and it's not likely I can do any either," Luke said with a smile. Luke suddenly realized the time and told Sue they had better leave now if they were going to be home on time.

Once in the car Luke realized he felt more calm and confident than he had earlier in the evening. He thought Sue might be sitting a little closer than before.

"Sue, would it be all right if we went out again soon? I don't know when I can use the car again but I'd like to spend more time with you."

Sue turned and smiled that smile that made him wonder if there could possibly be a more beautiful girl in all the world. "Of course I'd like to go out with you again. Call me when you have the car and we can talk," she said, as they pulled up in front of the house.

"Let me walk you to the door," Luke said as he got out of the car and hastily moved to open her door. They walked to the house side by side. Luke noticed that the house lights were all off except for the porch light over their heads.

"Thanks again, Sue. I had a wonderful time."

Sue turned to face him and Luke bent down and lightly kissed her on the lips. The kiss lasted only a second but it seemed that everything was a blur to Luke. As he turned to leave, he was confused. When he reached the car he turned and Sue was just opening the front door. She looked at Luke and waved, making him feel that what had just happened wasn't all bad. He got into the car with a little more confidence, but when he thought of how pretty Sue was and how many friends she had, he began to wonder if she could ever like him as much as he was beginning to like her.

Soon Luke pulled into his driveway. Sam was there to greet him, obviously happy to see him. Luke wasn't usually away from home this late and Sam didn't like any change in the routine. Luke petted Sam for a few minutes and then walked inside. All was quiet and Luke took off his shoes and slowly made his way upstairs. He shared his bedroom with his two brothers. They all had single beds and Jay and Gus were asleep. Luke quickly took his clothes off, laid them on his chair, and crawled into bed.

He lay there for a time thinking of his first date. He wished he had done some things differently, maybe made some witty comments that he hadn't thought of at the time, but he felt that Sue had had a good time and she seemed to like him at least a little. With that thought he fell asleep, content that he had acted respectfully and hadn't done anything to be ashamed of.

Chapter  3

Luke could have slept in a little on Sunday morning but he felt surprisingly rested and alert when he awoke at five o'clock. The sun was glowing orange in the eastern sky as he came out of the house and was instantly greeted by Sam, tail and rear end wagging so much he could hardly stand. As Luke petted Sam and calmed him down, he wondered if Sam actually was that glad to see him after just seeing him last night, or maybe dogs don't realize how much time elapses and to them it's the same if you're gone for one hour or one week. At any rate, Luke was grateful that he pleased Sam so much just by being there.

Sam was a stocky, muscular and powerful dog with a big head and short, dark brown hair. Al thought he might have some pit bull in him but he was much bigger than any pit bull Luke had seen. Sam had always been a gentle dog but was protective of the farm and family. Sam walked beside Luke as he hurried through his chores, then followed as Luke walked through the cow pasture, crossed the fence, and headed northeast. Luke walked slower than normal as he was in deep thought about last night. Sam kept himself busy with the sights, sounds, and smells of the new day. A chipmunk darted for the cover of a brush pile with Sam in deadly pursuit. Sam failed to find the little critter, even after whining, barking, and extensive digging. Soon he tired of this and ran to catch up to Luke, who was casually making his way to the creek.

Once he came to the embankment that overlooked the creek, Luke sat down and watched the creek. The sun was now sufficiently high and illuminated the creek as it turned abruptly at the embankment, forming a deep pocket in the creek bed. As he peered lazily into the water he could see a medium-sized trout rise to take an invisible insect floating on the surface. Sam sat down next to Luke, leaning heavily on Luke to achieve the physical contact that delighted him so much. Soon Sam lay down and Luke also lay down, using Sam's back for a pillow as he looked at the clear blue sky. Luke wondered if he was in love. He had never felt this way before, but he had never been very close to a girl besides his sisters, so he was a little confused. Sam sensed that Luke was acting abnormally, but was reveling in the time that Luke spent so close to him.

After some time had passed, Luke looked at his watch, got up, dusted off his jeans and started home.

"It's time to go back, Sam. I've got to go to church soon." He began to run at a quick pace toward home, Sam easily matching him stride for stride. He got home in time to inhale a bowl of cereal before he showered and dressed for church.

As the car pulled out of the driveway with the whole family packed in, Sam took up his position as sentinel and protector of the farm.

"We're going to be late again," Martha said to nobody in particular, just stating a fact. It was almost impossible to get to Sunday school but it didn't seem right that it would continually be a struggle to get to church without rushing. The small, white country church came into view as the car turned onto Hatch Road. The sun shone brilliantly on the roof and steeple. Several people were in front of the church talking as some were making their way into the church.

As the car pulled up to the church, Luke noticed Larry leaning against the railing at the top of the steps leading into the church.

"How's it going?" Luke asked as he joined Larry and they went into the church together.

"How'd it go last night?" Larry asked, his dark brown eyes darting from one of Luke's eyes to the other. Luke blushed, partially because of surprise but also because he couldn't stop thinking about Sue, even now.

"It went good," he answered cheerfully.

"It went well," Martha interrupted. This made Luke blush even more as he looked at his mother, who was also smiling as Luke quickened his pace into church.

The family sat together and took up a whole pew, with Luke and Larry on the end. Pastor Norton preached after the usual hymn singing, special solo, and announcements. Luke tried to keep his mind on the sermon but found it particularly hard today.

After the closing prayer they made their way out of the church. Larry and Luke were discussing their plans for the afternoon when they finally made their way beyond the doors and met the outstretched hand of Pastor Norton. He was a tall, thin man who always smiled, except when he was preaching, it seemed. He looked through his glasses down at the boys.

"How are you young men doing today?"

"Fine, Pastor," they said in unison.

"We're going to get together this next week with the youth group from Volinia Baptist. Can you come?" Pastor Norton asked.

"I think so, if I can get my chores done early enough," Luke said.

"Tuesday at eight P.M., here at the church," the pastor said cheerily. Then he was shaking hands with the people behind Luke and Larry.

Luke and Larry made plans to meet after dinner and then they got in their cars and left. Larry already had his own car and would have taken Luke home, except that he had to go to town. It was only a ten-minute drive home and everyone was hungry, knowing Martha made Sunday dinner a special meal. Luke had smelled the pies baking earlier as he got ready for church.

As they pulled into the driveway, Luke wondered where Sam was. Sam always was there to greet the family. As Al parked the car, everybody piled out and started for the house. Al stayed back with Luke. Luke called for Sam, but Sam didn't come. They walked into the barn and there was Brownie, who stretched, wagged his tail, and moved toward Al and Luke.

"Where's Sam?" Al asked Brownie, not really knowing why he even asked, except that he was getting nervous. Quickly they looked in each of the outbuildings and around the machinery, but there was no sign of Sam. Sam had vanished, just like several other neighborhood dogs before him.

As Al and Luke walked back toward the house, they met the other children. They had been looking for Sam also. When they went inside they found out that Martha had called the county sheriff's office, who put her in contact with the animal control officer. She gave him a description of Sam and he promised to be on the alert for any dogs of Sam's description coming into the pound. He told her to call back Monday, if Sam wasn't found, because they would have more staff on duty.

"What can we do, Dad?" Luke asked, his voice cracking with emotion.

"Let's eat dinner and think this over," Al said.

Although everyone said they weren't hungry, they consumed dinner in short order, discussing many questions and theories about Sam's disappearance.

"Sam must have been stolen," Luke finally said. "He'd never leave this property unless somebody took him."

Chapter 3

"You may be right," Al said, "but he wouldn't willingly leave with a stranger either."

There really were no answers and Luke had a sick feeling that Sam was gone forever. Larry came over and they walked around the whole section surrounding Luke's property, periodically calling for Sam, but there was no sign of him. They even walked on each side of the creek, upstream and downstream for a mile, thinking he somehow might have got caught or trapped. But there was no trace of Sam anywhere. Finally, they turned back toward the home.

"Maybe he'll be home when we get there," Larry said, trying to lift Luke's spirits, but Luke didn't even answer. When they got home, Sam was not there to greet them. The boys walked into the house and the children immediately deluged them with questions. Al was on the phone and motioned for quiet while he listened.

"Thanks, Harold. I'll let you know what happens," he said, hanging up the phone. He explained to the family, gathered in the dining room, that Harold Murphy, their nearest neighbor, had seen a truck in their driveway when he drove by with his tractor while they were at church. Harold had described the truck as a full-sized red pickup with a box on the back, like coon hunters have to keep their dogs in while traveling. Harold just assumed somebody was visiting and never gave it another thought, until Al called to ask if he had seen Sam.

It was now becoming clear that somebody knew that no one would be home during church and that was probably the best time to take Sam.

"But Sam wouldn't go with strangers," Luke said, knowing Sam's protective nature.

"Why would anyone want to take Sam?" Jay asked.

A silence seemed to last for minutes. Finally, Al got up and went toward the kitchen. "I don't know, Jay, but I know someone who might be able to help us." He opened a drawer and rooted around. "Where's our address book?"

Martha went to the drawer and Al moved aside. In seconds she had found the book. "Who are you looking for, dear?"

"See if you can find Jack's number in there," Al said, "I know he can help us."

Martha called the kids into the kitchen so Al could talk on the phone without interruption.

"Why does Dad think Uncle Jack can help?" Luke asked. "We really don't even know him. We hardly ever see him."

"I'll let your father explain," Martha said. "Just be quiet so your father can talk without interruptions." There was silence in the kitchen so that everyone could hear Al as he spoke to his brother. After a very short conversation Al hung up. The younger kids rushed into the dining room.

"Can he come?" Sandra asked. "I want Sam back."

"Yes, he can come," Al said. "He's between assignments and has time off," he said talking to his wife more than to the children. The children gradually dispersed, leaving Larry, Luke, and Luke's parents in the room together.

"Why do you think Uncle Jack can help us, Dad?" Luke asked.

Al hesitated for a few moments before answering. "I can't tell you all the details because Jack isn't allowed to speak much about what he does, so it's best not to ask him about that. But he does know certain things that may help us find Sam. Jack said he was going to come for a short visit anyway, so it worked out perfectly."

"Tell us about Uncle Jack," Luke pleaded. He didn't know anything about his uncle except that he was always busy with his work.

"Well, you know Jack's my little brother," Al began. "He's in his thirties now. I doubt you knew he was an all-state wrestler at a hundred and fifty-six pounds in his junior year, and state champion at a hundred and seventy-six pounds in his senior year of high school. He went to college on a scholarship but decided to join the Marines after his first year of college. He can maybe tell you about his Marine days, although he's very private about most of his life."

"What did he do after he got out of the Marines?" Larry asked. Both Luke and Larry were quite taken with Jack's life, especially Luke, having just seen his friend Ed the night before.

"Jack was in the Marines for several years before he left and went to work out east. Jack doesn't talk about his work and when pushed, just says it is classified. I think he just doesn't want people to get involved with him because his work may involve danger to him and possibly anyone close to him. That may be why he hasn't married," Al said, reflecting on their early life together and realizing that they had grown far apart through the years since childhood.

"When will he be here?" Luke asked.

"He's going to load up his pickup camper and start out tomorrow morning. He'll be here tomorrow evening, depending on when he gets started," Al said.

"Where's he going to stay?" Martha asked.

"He'll stay in his camper. That's the way he likes it," Al said, knowing they had no place for visitors to sleep except on the couch, which pulled out into a hide-a-bed. "We'd better get started on chores. It's getting late."

Luke and Larry went to start chores while the younger boys prepared for milking the cows. Luke felt more hopeful, but wished Uncle Jack could get here sooner, although he wasn't sure what he could find that hadn't been found already, which was nothing.

"What are you going to do after high school?" Larry asked Luke suddenly.

"I don't know. Why do you ask ?"

"I'm just wondering if I should apply for college or go into a branch of the service. My dad was in the Navy but only for three years during Viet Nam. He didn't see any real action and said he didn't like the Navy much," Larry said.

"I don't think I'll have enough money to go to college," Luke stated. "I know my grades aren't good enough for a scholarship and I can't go out for sports."

"How was your Uncle Jack able to go out for sports if he grew up on a farm too?" Larry asked.

"My Dad and Uncle Mark told Grandpa they would do more work if Uncle Jack could go out for the wrestling team. They knew he was pretty good and they wanted to give him the chance, and Grandpa said okay." Luke remembered that his dad said several times that Jack was a good wrestler because he was constantly beating Mark and him.

Larry and Luke finished Luke's chores and decided to take another look around the farm in case they had missed anything. As the boys walked toward the granery Luke spotted something orange in the grass. He motioned to Larry, who was closer, and he picked it up.

"It's some kind of dart," Larry stated in a matter-of-fact tone, "but what's it doing here?" There was a little blood on the needle end, which was hollow.

"Let's show this to Dad," Luke said, thinking it might be important. Al was in the milking parlor, changing milkers as the boys arrived. Luke quickly showed his dad the dart. He examined it for several seconds.

"It's a dart all right and it looks like it could carry some chemical inside, maybe a tranquilizer. Go to the house and give it to Mom to put away until Jack gets here."

The boys gave the dart to Martha and went back out by the granery to see if they could find anything else. The ground was still damp from the rain a couple of days ago. Luke couldn't make much of the tracks he saw but decided to make everyone stay away from the granery area until Uncle Jack came. It was getting dark and Larry had to leave but promised to come back tomorrow if his folks would let him. Usually his folks let Larry do whatever he wanted, as they both worked.

Luke went into the house and made a peanut butter and jelly sandwich. He got a glass of fresh milk from the refrigerator and looked in the cupboard until he found where his mom had put the dart. She had sealed it in a Tupperware container. Luke decided not to open the container, afraid he might mess up the evidence somehow, so he closed the cupboard and took his sandwich and milk to the dining room table. Martha, sitting in an arm chair not far away, was sewing a dress for one of the girls.

"Do you think Uncle Jack can really help?" Luke asked, a sense of urgency in his voice.

"I don't know Jack that well myself," Martha said, "but I know he has worked with law enforcement people and seems to hold his job, whatever that is. Remember not to ask too many questions or Jack will just clam up and maybe won't even help find Sam." This statement made Luke very nervous so he decided not to ask his uncle any personal questions if he could help it.

Luke told his mom and dad goodnight and went upstairs to bed. He felt very tired, probably because of his short night last night and all the confusion associated with Sam's disappearance today. He lay down on the bed and immediately fell asleep.

Chapter 4

Luke woke up promptly at 5:05 A.M. He went to the window to see if Sam had miraculously returned. He didn't see Sam but was very surprised to see a full-sized, green Chevrolet pickup with a big white camper on it.

"Uncle Jack!" Luke shouted, not meaning to talk out loud. Jay and Gus didn't move—they never woke until their parents got them up—but Martha and Al must have heard Luke as there was stirring in their bedroom. Luke quickly dressed and went downstairs to use the bathroom. He washed his hands and face hurriedly and would have let it go at that but a quick glance in the mirror showed him his hair was a mess. He held his head under the faucet until his hair was all wet. Then he dried it with a towel and combed it straight back. He then made his way to the kitchen, where Martha was making coffee.

"Don't go out right now," she said, reading her son's mind. "Jack must have traveled all night to get here. Maybe he'll sleep for awhile."

Al ventured into the kitchen and took the cup of coffee Martha had made. He looked tired and always limped for a little while after he got up.

"I wonder why Jack came so soon?" he asked, taking a sip of the hot brew.

"He probably knew how much Sam means to the children," Martha said. The three of them sat at the table and drank coffee in silence, trying to wake up and get their brains and bodies functioning for the day ahead. Soon they heard a door close outside.

Jack came in through the mud room and gave a quick knock before opening the kitchen door.

"Jack, how good of you to come!" Martha exclaimed, reaching up to give him a hug.

"Glad to see you, Sis," Jack said, somewhat bashfully.

"How have you been, Jack?" Al asked. "You're looking good."

"I've been well. I was just taking my first vacation in a year and was wondering what I was going to do when you called," Jack explained. "I couldn't sleep so I decided to drive until I got tired, but I never got tired." He shook Al's hand. "And this must be Luke. It's been a while since I've seen him."

Luke reached out his right hand to shake, but Jack grabbed it and pulled Luke to him for a big hug. Luke was a little embarrassed but managed a red-faced smile. "Thanks for coming, Uncle Jack."

"You must have grown a foot since I last saw you," Jack exclaimed. "How long has it been?"

"At least three years, Jack," Al said.

"It doesn't seem possible. Where does time go?" Jack asked, more to himself than anybody in particular.

"Have a seat, Jack. Martha just made some coffee. Have you had any breakfast?" Al asked.

"Breakfast sounds great, brother. Driving seems to stimulate my appetite."

As the two brothers got caught up on their lives Luke observed Jack. He was probably six feet tall or so, of medium build, with dark brown hair and eyes, and a day's growth of whiskers. Somehow Luke had envisioned him differently, possibly like Arnold Schwarzenegger and maybe a bit taller; instead he was looking at an average man.

Before long, Martha had made bacon and eggs with fried potatoes and they were all eating. The small talk continued until they had finished breakfast and Jack leaned back in his chair with a cup of coffee.

"Well, what do you think happened to your dog?" he asked.

Al told him about the disappearances of neighborhood dogs, Sam's disappearance, and Luke's finding the dart. He fetched the dart and handed it to Jack. Jack sat upright and studied it intently for a full minute.

"It's a dart that's shot from a tranquilizer gun using a .22 blank to propel it. When the dart hits the animal, the chemical is injected through the needle, just like from a normal syringe," he said finally.

Luke was slightly surprised at his knowledge and listened intently.

Jack continued. "Often the dart is loaded with a mixture of Rompun and Telazol. If shot into a muscle, a dog will be out cold in three to five minutes and will sleep for several hours. Show me where you found this, Luke."

"He can show you later, Jack. You need some rest," Martha said.

Jack laughed, kidding her about her mothering instincts, and then assured her he was fine. When Jack had finished talking to Martha, Luke got up and led the way to the door.

"I found it out by the granery," he told Jack as they walked together to where he had found the dart. Jack started looking around, bending very close to the earth, squatting down several times, but not saying anything. After several minutes he stood upright and walked back up the driveway, stopping several times to look at the ground—for tire marks, Luke thought.

Jack walked up and down the driveway slowly and methodically. Luke could hear the sounds of his dad starting to milk the cows. Luke was just about to tell Jack he had to do his chores when Jack finally spoke.

"It looks to me like the truck came in and parked in the driveway. Sam probably came out to bark and circle the truck. Someone put the tranquilizer gun out the window and shot Sam. But Sam is a big dog and didn't get completely tranquilized. He wandered toward the granery and they followed in the truck, shot him again and then loaded him in the truck and took off. Of course, I'm only guessing at some of this, but I found a couple drops of blood back in the driveway, probably where he was shot the first time. There are tire tracks leading back here, but there are so many other tracks I can't make out the tire brand of the truck. Once they got Sam loaded they probably forgot to pick up the second dart before they took off."

"Who would take Sam, Uncle Jack?" Luke asked.

"Judging from Sam's description, my guess is someone is training fighting dogs and Sam looked like a good prospect," Jack stated in a factual manner.

Luke was dying to ask how he knew so much but remembered what his dad had said about asking questions. "How can we find him? Do you think he's still alive?" Luke blurted out.

"I can't tell if he's still alive but I would guess so, although I don't know how long he will be alive. It may depend on his ability to fight for survival," Jack said. "It's going to take a little doing, but I think we can find out where these dogs are being taken. You go do your chores and I'll make some phone calls." Luke turned back to see Jack greet Gus and Jay as they came out to help with milking. He hugged them both and talked for a few minutes before going inside.

Luke did his chores as fast as he could without being sloppy, as that was against his nature. His dad and mom had taught him that it was a sacred responsibility to care for the farm animals and each animal was treated with respect. Finishing up, Luke went to the house to see if Jack had been able to make his calls. Jack was talking to Nancy and Sandra, telling them how much they'd grown. He looked up when Luke came in.

"My friend's office doesn't open until eight o'clock so we have to wait a few more minutes." Jack then started talking to Martha while the girls listened intently.

Luke's mind wandered as he tried to figure out how Jack planned to find Sam. It seemed so hopeless, even with the information Jack had already gleaned from his observations. His feelings wavered between confident and hopeless, but he felt mostly hopeless. He would have to rely totally on Jack, but he wanted to help in any way he could.

Finally eight o'clock arrived and Jack made the phone call. Luke didn't feel comfortable listening to the conversation but it sounded as though Jack was talking to a doctor about some technical stuff. When Jack came back into the kitchen Al and the younger boys were coming in from chores. Mom asked the smaller children to go into the living room. Jack quickly explained his plan.

"We're dealing with professional dog thieves, I think," he began. "Most law enforcement agencies don't get very involved because there are few clues, and human lives are not at stake, so it is a low-priority crime. I just talked to a friend of mine, a veterinarian, and he said he'd be willing to do minor surgery to insert a tracking device in a dog I'll take to him. Then we can use that dog as bait. If the thieves take that dog, we can track them. My guess is that they're not keeping these dogs anywhere close because this area is not isolated enough to harbor many dogs without their barking drawing attention. Even if they're not keeping the dogs long but stealing them to sell to laboratories, they have to travel to bigger cities to deliver them."

Luke felt a lump develop in his throat. He had never thought about Sam being used in experiments. He tried to suppress tears but they welled up in his eyes. Jack put a hand on his shoulder and squeezed firmly.

"Look at me, Luke," Jack ordered. Through tears, Luke looked up at him. "None of this is going to be simple or easy, but I want you to know that I'll do my best and work as fast as possible so that we have the best chance of saving Sam, but I need you to be strong."

"I'll do anything to save Sam," Luke said with conviction. "I want to help you find him." He looked at his dad, knowing it was ultimately his parents' decision.

"We'll discuss that as things develop," Al said. "Where are you going to get a dog to use as bait?" he asked.

"From what you have told me, the thieves are looking for young, big, muscular dogs. I'll go up to Kalamazoo and see what they have at the Humane Society. Once I find a dog that has a lot of the physical characteristics we're looking for, I'll 'adopt' him and take him to my friend to get the tracking device implanted. It will take awhile for the incision to heal but during that time we'll have the dog here and the word will get out that you have another dog. These thieves are quite bold and they'll come again if they feel they got away with it before."

"Jack, you don't have time for all this!" Martha interrupted.

"I have a lot of vacation time coming and this will be a great time to get to know my nieces and nephews better. Right now, I need to take the camper off the truck, take a shower and go find a dog."

"How long will you be gone?" Luke asked, worried that each passing day would lower Sam's chances.

"I'll stop in Kalamazoo first and then go on to Lansing, to my veterinarian friend. I'll probably leave the dog overnight and then bring him here tomorrow, if all goes well. I'll need to park the camper out of the way, so as not to draw attention, but I need to plug it in to an electrical outlet."

"You can park it up close to the back porch," Al explained. "There's a plug-in there and the camper can't be seen from the road."

"Sounds good," Jack said cheerfully. "Let's unload the camper so I can get started."

Luke had more questions but didn't want to take up valuable time. He could probably get those questions answered when Uncle Jack returned. Luke was still worried for Sam's life but he sensed a confidence in Jack that made him feel more hopeful.

Chapter 5

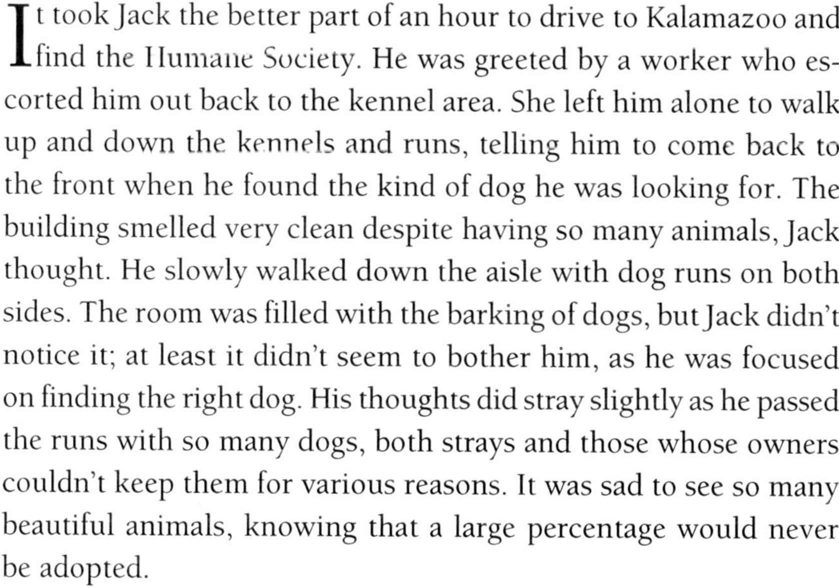

It took Jack the better part of an hour to drive to Kalamazoo and find the Humane Society. He was greeted by a worker who escorted him out back to the kennel area. She left him alone to walk up and down the kennels and runs, telling him to come back to the front when he found the kind of dog he was looking for. The building smelled very clean despite having so many animals, Jack thought. He slowly walked down the aisle with dog runs on both sides. The room was filled with the barking of dogs, but Jack didn't notice it; at least it didn't seem to bother him, as he was focused on finding the right dog. His thoughts did stray slightly as he passed the runs with so many dogs, both strays and those whose owners couldn't keep them for various reasons. It was sad to see so many beautiful animals, knowing that a large percentage would never be adopted.

One yellow lab cross seemed to focus on Jack as he walked by. Jack looked back at him a couple times just to see if the dog was still watching, which he was. It wasn't the type of dog Jack was looking for and with his work he couldn't have a dog of his own, but he felt sorry for this creature who seemed to be trying to communicate with him.

He continued walking down the aisle, dogs still barking on both sides, and came to a rather large, short-haired, stocky dog with light brown hair, lying quietly back at the far end of the run. Jack looked at the card on the kennel door: "Buster." He squatted down and tried to get the dog's attention, calling his name, whistling and snapping his fingers. The dog lifted his eye lids and stared at Jack, not moving any other body part, not even his tail. Yes, this dog had promise. He had the physical characteristics Jack was looking for but didn't seem overly friendly, which was okay, as long as Jack could handle him.

Jack continued his search until he was satisfied that he had seen every dog. He then walked back to the front office and asked about Buster. The worker, a middle-aged woman with graying hair, went through a small stack of files until she found the right file.

"He comes from a couple who had to move to an apartment that would not take pets," she explained. "Buster is a healthy dog, four years old and has been neutered. He has all his vaccinations and is described as a loyal family pet with good temperament."

Taking Jack back to the kennel area, she got a leash, unlocked the run door, and called for Buster to come. The dog stood and slowly walked toward the worker. She snapped the leash onto the collar, brought the dog out of the run, handed the leash to Jack, and told Jack to follow her. The dog came along obediently to a quiet exercise area where Jack and Buster could get acquainted. The worker left, saying she would return in ten or fifteen minutes.

Jack reached down and petted Buster, who did not bother to look up or acknowledge Jack in any way. Jack tried to see if the dog knew any commands. When he was told to sit, Buster immediately sat down on his rear legs. He also responded to "Come," but didn't seem to know much else, which was fine with Jack, as long as he wasn't adopting a viscous dog, which he was convinced was not the case. Jack felt that Buster was just lonesome for the people he had lived with for most of his life.

Chapter 5

When the worker came back Jack told her he wanted Buster. Jack soon found that these workers are required to ask many questions about the new home the dog will be moving into. Jack told her that Buster would be living on a farm with five children and would receive a lot of attention. The worker, having asked all her questions and being satisfied with Jack's answers, had him come to the front, leading Buster. Jack then paid the adoption fee and got all the paperwork concerning Buster's vaccinations and most recent exam. He was allowed to keep the leash because he had forgot to bring one. He also gave some extra money so that the yellow lab-cross could stay longer than was normal, with hope of finding a good home for him.

Jack walked out with Buster, opened the passenger door of the truck and commanded Buster to jump in, which he did without hesitating. He sat on the floor. After starting the truck and backing up, Jack glanced down at Buster, who was still on the floor but was looking intently at Jack. Jack motioned for him to get on the seat, which he quickly did. He then lay down, but kept his eyes on Jack as they started their journey.

The trip to Lansing went quickly. Jack used his cell phone to ask a friend to air express a tracking device and monitor to a vet in Lansing. It wouldn't arrive until tomorrow morning, so Jack called Al and told him not to expect him home before tomorrow night. This wasn't good news for Luke, but he was beginning to learn that patience is a good thing, especially when there is nothing else that can be done.

After finishing his phone calls, Jack endeavored to make friends with Buster, who continued to lie still on the seat, looking intently at him. While Jack talked to Buster he slowly put out his hand, being careful not to expose his fingers, allowing Buster to smell it as a long as he wished, and then slowly continued moving his hand until he was petting Buster on top of the head. Buster at least seemed to accept this and before long he moved his tail slightly.

Jack was encouraged by this and praised Buster, stroking his head and neck with more confidence. Jack didn't want to become too attached, but he wanted to be able to trust Buster to obey him and feel comfortable with him around his brother's children.

Jack continued to make friends until he pulled into the driveway of Miller Animal Clinic. As Jack opened the door to enter the waiting room, Buster suddenly stopped and began shaking. Jack knelt down and comforted him, and finally coaxed him inside.

"Dr. Miller is just finishing a surgery," the smiling receptionist told Jack. "He'll be with you in a few minutes." Jack took a seat. Across the room was a young woman with a cat in a carrier beside her. He smiled but the young woman seemed too concerned to smile back.

"Jack Larson, how are you doing?" The voice brought Jack back from his thoughts.

"How are you, Glenn? It's been awhile," Jack replied.

"Come into this exam room and let's talk."

Jack got up and Buster carefully followed with his tail between his legs. It was obvious Buster had been to a vet's office before, and certainly didn't like it very much.

Jack told the veterinarian the reason for the visit after the two men got caught up on each other's lives. Glenn did most of the talking because he knew Jack couldn't say much about himself, except in generalities. Glenn also knew Jack was honest and would not mistreat Buster, and so he agreed to surgically insert a tracking device into Buster.

"How big is this device?" he asked.

"About as big as a fifty-cent piece," Jack replied. "You can make a small incision in the middle of the back, by the shoulders and put it between the skin and muscle."

"That should be easy enough. Leave Buster with me and we'll get him ready for surgery tomorrow."

Chapter 5

"One other thing, Glenn. Don't shave the hair, as that might raise some questions," Jack reminded Glenn.

"That's not a problem. If the tracker comes tomorrow morning we'll put it in right away and Buster should be ready to travel by afternoon. I'll use a sedative and a local so he won't be so tired when you pick him up."

"Thanks, Glenn. This means a lot to me," Jack said. "Give my regards to Alice. I'll see you tomorrow around two o'clock or so." With that, Jack handed Buster's leash to the vet, who was already making friends with Buster. Jack knew he was in good hands and that he could trust Glenn to be confidential about this matter.

Jack quickly found a motel and took a two-hour nap. Then he got up, showered, ate a small lunch, and went to the Potter Park Zoo, partially to relax but also to get some questions answered. Dr. Miller had promised to call the veterinarian on staff at the zoo and arrange for Jack to talk to her. After paying his admission he went to the office to see if he could find the vet. He was informed that Dr. Smith was in the cat house but was expecting Jack. As he followed directions to the cat house he passed some ostriches, giraffes, and a rhinoceros, all beautiful creatures and obviously well cared for. Soon Jack was at the entrance to the cat house. Inside, other patrons were milling around watching zoo personnel perform some task. Jack was unable to tell exactly what was happening and soon a cover was drawn over the glass so people couldn't see what was being done.

Jack spotted a door marked Employees Only, and knocked. A petite, twenty-something woman in oversize green coveralls immediately opened the door. Jack explained that Dr. Smith was expecting him and the woman asked him to wait while she checked. Soon she invited Jack inside and escorted him to a small area where a group of three people were standing. As Jack approached, a very pretty lady with short blond hair stuck out her hand.

"I'm Jeanette Smith," she stated with a quick smile. "Glenn told me you wanted to talk. Right now we're waiting for the 'kitty dentist' to arrive. Then we're going to dart a Siberian tiger and fix his tooth. I don't do root canals but a local veterinary dental specialist does, so he's coming by soon. He's been slightly delayed, so your timing is perfect."

Jack looked intently at Dr. Smith, thinking that she obviously loved her work, felt confident about her abilities, and knew her limitations.

"How will you anesthetize the tiger?" he asked after thanking her for taking the time to talk to him.

"We'll use a tranquilizer dart to immobilize him and then use gas anesthesia to maintain him while the doctor does the root canal."

Jack showed her the dart that had been used to tranquilize Sam. She recognized it immediately. "They come in various sizes, from lcc to 5cc. The smaller darts are more accurate so we sometimes 'boil down' the drugs to concentrate them so we can use the smaller syringe. You then use a syringe and needle to push the tranquilizer into the dart. Then seal the needle with a little petroleum jelly and you're ready to go." Dr. Smith showed Jack the tranquilizer gun, which was all ready to use on the tiger. "Anyone can buy these guns and darts from the manufacturer, but the chemicals have to come from a veterinarian, unless they are obtained illegally."

"This helps a great deal, doctor. Thanks so much for your time," Jack said as he got up to leave. "Oh, what if one syringe doesn't tranquilize the animal adequately?"

"That happens more frequently than I care to admit," Dr. Smith said. "You then have to literally guess how much more to give, depending on how alert the animal is. It's not very scientific, but usually works out well."

Chapter 5

"What do you use on members of the canine family?" Jack asked.

"A combination of Rompun and Telazol," Dr. Smith said in matter-of-fact fashion.

"One last question," Jack shyly asked, hoping to not wear out his welcome. "How do you know this tiger needs a root canal?"

"Come here and let me show you," Dr. Smith said as she moved to a bigger room where a beautiful Siberian tiger was caged. It was a very small cage, designed so that the big cat could not move around much. As the two approached, the cat opened his mouth and showed his teeth. The upper right canine tooth was broken off about one inch from the tip. Dr. Smith explained that if a root canal wasn't done the tooth would probably become infected sometime in the future. "It's better to fix it now than extract it later," she stated in her jovial voice.

After thanking her again Jack was ushered out by the young lady with the over-sized coveralls. "Have a good time at our zoo," she said as she closed the door. Jack could hear the lock click behind him as he walked through the main lobby of the cat house. Jack was impressed by the neatness of the facility and the obvious good health of the animals. Dr. Smith and her crew obviously took pride in their work.

Jack hadn't really learned a lot he didn't already know but he did feel that he was correct in the method used to steal Sam. After leaving the zoo, Jack went out for supper, although most of his friends called it dinner. He had a salad and a salmon steak with some vegetables. He wasn't really hungry but knew he'd better eat something before returning to the motel.

The next morning Jack was up early, as was his custom. He kept a small New Testament with him when he traveled, and read it regularly every day. He would then pray for several minutes before beginning his workout. He had a home gym that worked fine when he was home but while on the road he mostly did calisthenics, which consisted of pull-ups, push-ups, various types of sit-ups, jumping jacks, stretching exercises, and a two—to four-mile run, depending on the time available. Having done this, he showered and went out for breakfast, which usually consisted of oatmeal, skimmed milk, orange juice, and dry toast or half of a plain bagel, a far cry from what Martha fed him, he thought.

After breakfast Jack called Dr. Miller to make sure the tracking device had arrived. It had, so Jack explained how to check and make sure the device worked properly. Having done this, Jack was satisfied that he had done what he needed to prepare for taking Buster home. He went back to the motel for a quick swim before checking out and going to pick up Buster.

At the clinic, the receptionist invited Jack to go back to where Dr. Miller was doing surgery. He followed her down the hall and through a double door into a treatment room, where an anesthetic machine was sitting idle. She motioned Jack to follow through another double door, where Glenn was performing surgery on a fairly large dog. The vet wore a cap, surgical gloves, and gown, and a surgical drape covered the dog completely except for his head and the surgical area. A technician was monitoring anesthesia but no one assisted Glenn as he worked inside the abdomen of this dog.

"Hi, Jack," Glenn said cheerily. "Your dog is about ready to go. Everything went fine. Just as I was finishing Buster, this guy was brought in. He was hit by a car and has a ruptured spleen." Glenn worked with a speed and skill that set him apart from other veterinarians. He had a God-given gift and was at his best in these situations.

"You don't need me to scrub in and help, do you, Glenn?" Jack said, laughing.

"I'm doing fine," Glenn laughed. "I wouldn't want to worry about you passing out on me during surgery!" Both men laughed.

Dr. Miller asked another technician to get Buster and take him to the reception area.

"Thanks so much, Glenn. I'll tell you what this is all about sometime."

"No problem," Glenn stated, but don't forget the other part of the tracking device. It's in my office on my desk. Just get it as you're on your way out."

"Thanks again, Glenn." Jack found the device, made sure it was in working order, and then went to the waiting room, where he was greeted by a very tired Buster; who nonetheless was happy to see him and wearily wagged his tail.

"How's it going, boy?" Jack asked. "Looks like you'll sleep well tonight."

"I'd like to pay my bill," Jack said, turning to the receptionist.

"Dr. Miller said there was no charge, Mr. Larson."

Jack had anticipated this. He handed an envelope to the receptionist. He had $150 in it with a card, thanking him again for all his help.

"Come on, boy, let's go home." Buster sensed he was leaving this God-forsaken place and wasted no time getting to the door. Jack didn't want to pull on the leash for fear it might hurt Buster's incision, but Buster seemed to be in no pain. He just wanted to be out of this place!

Buster was able to put his front feet up unto the floor of the truck but needed Jack's assistance to get his other half up. Then Jack had to help get Buster situated on the truck seat, where he finally relaxed and slept all the way to the Larson farm.

Chapter  6

Wake up Buster, we're home, Jack said as he pulled into the driveway. Buster opened his eyes and stretched, still tired from the sedative. Suddenly he became alert as new smells entered his olfactory apparatus. The smells of the farm intrigued him, and he wanted to explore these new smells to their source. Buster had already learned to trust Jack. Dogs are usually better judges of character than people. Jack didn't know how Buster would react to children, and he was about to find out, as the whole family came out to meet them.

Sandra started to walk toward Buster but Jack stopped her. "I don't know if Buster has played with young people," he explained, but Buster wagged his tail and walked toward Sandra, begging to be petted. Soon all the children were kneeling beside Buster, and the dog loved it.

"I hope they don't get too attached," Jack said to his brother. "If our plan works, he'll be taken within two weeks and we'll be on our way to finding Sam and the people who took him."

"Are these people dangerous?" Al asked with some concern in his voice.

"I suppose anyone can be considered dangerous if he's cornered," Jack said, "but it's not likely that it would get out of control. I just don't know for sure who we're up against, though."

That said, they again focused on the children welcoming their new friend into the family. Jack cautioned everyone to avoid the area around the shoulder where there were some sutures, even though it took a trained eye to part the hair and find where the transmitter had been placed.

"Oh, my!" Martha exclaimed. "My soup is going to burn. It's almost time for lunch everyone. You children come in and get cleaned up and ready to eat."

Buster was allowed to come into the mud room while everyone ate. No pet was ever allowed in the Larson house, even though they were all loved and well cared for. Even having an animal in the mud room was unusual but Martha knew the kids would not eat their lunch properly if the dog were tied outside. Soon everyone was seated and Al prayed, thanking God for Jack's safety as well as for the food. It was always very quiet during the blessing of the meal, Jack thought, and then it was almost comical the way the children began talking simultaneously as soon as their father said, "Amen." Of course, the conversation centered on Buster, who seemed to make an instant hit with everyone; everyone but Luke, who purposely didn't pay too much attention to the new dog. Luke felt it wouldn't be right to be too excited about Buster so soon after Sam disappeared.

Soon the younger children finished and asked to be excused, each one going to the mud room to visit their new friend.

"You must be tired after doing so much in the last couple of days," Martha said.

"It was actually refreshing," Jack replied. "I got a good night's sleep. Everything went very smoothly."

Implying that Jack was tired was merely an opening for conversation, because as long as Martha had known Jack, he never acted tired, or hungry, or thirsty; if anything bothered him, he never complained. Martha figured it was a part of his training, but also it was the way he had been raised from childhood, because her husband was very much like Jack in that he never complained.

Finally Luke worked up his courage and looked directly at Jack. "What's your plan?" He was somewhat embarrassed by his own boldness.

Jack smiled and looked directly into Luke's eyes. "I'll tell you my plan, Luke, but I need you to relax and be patient. This is going to take a little time but it's the only way I know to find Sam."

As Luke looked into Jack's eyes and heard what Jack said, a feeling that everything would be all right and Sam would return home came over him. It must have been the quiet confidence that Jack possessed.

Martha and Al engaged Jack in small talk for a while longer, and Luke was about to ask to be excused, when Jack finally turned to him.

"Let's go over the plan, Luke. I don't want the younger children to know anything about this, as they could inadvertently tell someone and spoil the plan. We're going to use Buster as bait. We'll get him used to these surroundings and then let him stay in the yard just like Sam. Buster is similar to Sam in body type and size so he must be what these people are looking for. Since little has been done to stop these people they won't hesitate to do the same thing again. Except this time they'll steal a dog with a radio transmitter embedded under his skin. We'll be able to track him as long as we stay in range of the signal. They'll lead us to where they keep these stolen dogs and we'll be able to get the local authorities to step in and break up this gang of thieves."

"It sounds like a good plan," Al said, after thinking for a few moments. "It doesn't sound like there is any danger in what you're doing. How will you follow them?"

"I'll take the truck and the camper, and tow a smaller four-wheel-drive vehicle, in case we have to go back into the woods further than the truck will go."

"I want to go with you, Uncle Jack," Luke stated in a voice of firm resolve that both Jack and Luke's parents could not deny.

"It shouldn't take more than a few days," Jack said. "What about the work load around the farm?"

"I think we can manage for a few days," Al said.

Martha interrupted, "But you must stay out of danger, even if you have to stop following these people."

"He'll be with me all the time," Jack promised. That statement alone seemed to be enough to satisfy Luke's parents.

"What do we do now?" Luke asked.

"We have a few preparations to make," Jack said, "but mostly, we wait. You're going to learn patience, Luke."

All three adults smiled, knowing the impatience of youth, but knowing the importance of that life lesson. The rest of the day was spent doing chores and all the jobs associated with the farm. With Buster on a leash, Jack walked around the yard, trying to familiarize the dog with his new surroundings. Even Brownie seemed to accept Buster as a new member of the family. After sniffing the newcomer tentatively for a few moments, Brownie went back and laid down in one of his beds that he had dug out of the earth under a shade tree.

Early the next morning Luke got up before his dad and brothers, as he often did, and went downstairs and got ready to do his chores. As he walked out the back door he was surprised to see Jack, who had spent the night in his camper, doing a series of calisthenics. He was just finishing, apparently, because he got up from some sort of stretching exercise and walked over to Luke.

"Good morning, Luke," Jack said as he wiped perspiration from his face and eyes with a small towel he had stuffed in his back pocket.

Chapter 6

"Why are you up so early, Uncle Jack?" Luke asked, wondering if something was going on.

"I guess being raised on the farm got me in the habit of getting up early," Jack said. "Buster spent the night in the mud room and I took him for a little walk. We'll be able to let him loose in a few days when he's acclimated to his new digs."

"Why are you sweating?" Luke asked, wondering if there was some special thing he was preparing for.

"I just have to do some exercises to keep me limber," Jack informed him. "I don't work hard like you and your dad, so I have to do something to stay in shape. I'm about to take a little run and then I'll come back and shower. You'll probably be done with your chores by then, right?"

"I should be," Luke said.

Jack jogged toward the gravel road and headed south at a brisk pace. Luke would have liked to run with him but was afraid to ask, and he had to do his chores anyway. During chores Luke kept thinking about his uncle. He had been surprised to find him awake and active so early in the morning, even when he didn't have chores to do. As Luke hustled through chores he saw Jack come back from his run. After resting for a moment Jack went over to the big maple tree in the front yard, jumped up and hung from one of the limbs, as if to stretch his body. Then he started doing pull-ups. Luke, if he counted right, saw Jack do twenty-five pull-ups before he again just hung by his hands from the tree and finally let go and dropped to the ground. He did some more stretching, and then, evidently satisfied with how he felt, walked toward his camper to take a shower. Luke was beginning to realize that Jack was a well-conditioned athlete who took physical fitness seriously. Luke knew better than to say anything about seeing Jack do those pull-ups, as it would probably embarrass him.

Soon Luke was done with his chores and headed to the house for breakfast. He stopped in the mud room to pet Buster for a few minutes, who seemed to enjoy the attention but laid fairly still. Martha had fixed oatmeal, so Luke washed and sat at the kitchen table. Breakfast was the one meal they did not eat as a family. It was done more or less in shifts, depending on how long chores took. As Luke sat waiting for his mother to dish up the oatmeal, Jack came in, fresh from his shower.

"Good morning, Martha," Jack said in a cheery, pleasant voice.

"I hope you like oatmeal, Jack?" Martha questioned.

"That sounds good to me," Jack stated as he sat down across from Luke.

"What are your plans today?" Luke asked as the oatmeal arrived.

"I have to stick around the house for a few days, as we need to get Buster used to the place. Once we're sure he won't run off, we'll let him stay outside. He's got to have a little time for that incision to heal, too, so we'll just take it slow for the next few days. Take some time to become friends with Buster, Luke, because it is important that he bonds with us."

Al, Gus, and Jay soon came in for breakfast. Most of the farm work was done for the day except for evening chores, so Al and Martha were going to drive into town with the children. Luke said he'd rather stay home. He decided to call Larry to see what he was doing and found out from his mother that he had gone to visit his sister for a few days. While he was still on the phone, the family filed past Luke on their way out.

Luke could see Jack through the back door, and decided he would try to get to know his uncle better, if he didn't mind. When Luke opened the back door Jack was just coming out of the camper with a carry case and a quiver with half a dozen arrows. "You don't mind if I shoot a few arrows, do you Luke?" Jack asked.

"Well, no, of course not," Luke said. "Do you want me to set up a couple bales of hay?"

"That would be great," Jack said. "I'll help. Let's put them over by the corn crib." Jack followed Luke into the upper part of the barn and soon they emerged with two bales of hay. After placing one bale on its side and the other on top of it, Luke followed Jack back to where he left his case and arrows.

Jack opened the soft green case and pulled out three pieces of wood, two of which had distinctive curves. Luke had never seen a bow like this. Jack grabbed the smaller piece of wood, which he called a riser, and quickly fitted the other two pieces onto it, making it look like a recurve bow. He then put a string on one end by a loop and did the same to the other end. He then pulled from his pocket another piece of rope with a piece of leather on each end. He put one of these on the tip of each end of the bow, stepped on the rope, which was lying on the ground, and pulled upward on the bow with his left hand while pushing the bow string to the tip of the bow until the loop rested in the notches at the tip of the bow. Now the bow was strung and ready to shoot.

Jack inspected the bow and flexed it several times until he seemed satisfied. Then he took an arrow from the quiver. Each of the six arrows had some sort of camouflage pattern with one red and two white feathers by the nock at the end. Luke looked at the bales and told Jack to wait. He picked up a small piece of paper and ran over to the bales. He placed the paper under the bale string close to the center of the upper bale and ran back.

"Now you have a target," Luke stated, satisfied that he had helped his uncle. The bales were perhaps twenty yards away and the paper was not much bigger than a post card. Jack put the arrow on the bow shelf and placed the nock of the arrow on the string. He turned and looked at the card briefly, methodically began drawing the bow as he raised it until his bow arm stiffened and he had the string drawn back to the corner of his mouth. In an instant the arrow was gone and Luke looked at the bales to see the arrow protruding from the card.

"You hit it," Luke said, not meaning to act so surprised. "How'd you do that? I have a couple of friends who have bows but they don't look like yours, and they have to aim with a sight, and their bow has wheels on each end."

"They're shooting compound bows," Jack explained. "This is a recurve bow. Some people even shoot what is called a long bow, like Robin Hood. I've been shooting a bow for years. I guess you could say it's my hobby. I do it to relax. I also hunt with it if I get a chance."

"Could I hold it?" Luke asked. Jack handed the bow to Luke, who grabbed it in his left hand, felt it balance there briefly, and then pulled back on the string. The string was hard to pull back but he finally managed, although he couldn't hold the bow still.

"This bow's a bit too heavy for you, Luke, but I've got a spare bow in the camper if you want to try a shot," Jack said. Luke assured Jack he was interested so Jack quickly went back to the camper and emerged with another recurve bow.

"This is a one-piece recurve. Mine is called a take-down, which makes it easy for traveling." He then put the bow stringer on each end of the bow and quickly strung the one-piece bow. "Here you go, Luke."

Luke pulled the string back on this bow with ease. "Can I shoot it?" he asked eagerly. He explained to Jack he had only shot a bow when he was little at a day camp and couldn't really remember what to do. Jack took an arrow out of the quiver. As Luke held the bow, Jack put his left hand over Luke's and placed the arrow on the shelf, or rest. He then nocked the arrow with the other hand.

"The arrow goes between these two nock points," he said, pointing to the area the nock now occupied. "I almost forgot," Jack said. "Put the bow down for a second and just pick a spot on the corn crib with your left hand." Luke picked a spot on the side of the corn crib where the paint was faded and Jack told him to keep pointing his finger at the spot.

Chapter 6

"Now close your right eye," Jack ordered. When Luke closed his right eye his finger was pointing far to the right of the spot. He told Jack what it looked like and then Jack told him to open the right eye and close the left. Now his finger was pointing at the faded spot, like it was with both eyes open.

"What does that mean?" Luke asked, confused by the testing.

"I needed to find which eye was dominant. Since you use your right eye to line up things you are pointing at, that is called your dominant eye. You would probably do better shooting right handed, because as you draw the arrow back it will be in line with the right eye," Jack explained in his patient way. "Now let's get closer to the bale so you can take a few shots." Jack went up to the bale and pulled out his arrow. They backed a few steps from the bale but Luke suddenly realized he didn't know a thing about drawing the bow and actually shooting an arrow. He faced the target briefly and then turned to Jack, with a questioning look.

Jack smiled. "I'm glad you didn't just shoot, Luke. It's important to have the proper form before you can even hope to shoot a bow accurately. Let me help you get started. Then you can decide if you want to continue." Jack described proper shooting form in detail to Luke. He had Luke stand properly with his feet spaced shoulder width apart, and showed him how to draw the bow, and anchor and release the string. After several minutes of instruction, Jack was satisfied that he had covered the basics. Then he walked over and took the paper off the bale.

"I want you to practice what I taught you, but don't even worry about being accurate. I want you to develop the proper form. If you do that, accuracy will come with practice."

Luke was anxious to get started but was a little confused. "I have a friend who shoots a compound bow, and he was shooting well an hour after we started. This seems harder."

"It's harder to learn, but the benefits of learning to shoot this way are so much greater, it's worth the effort. You can shoot at moving targets more easily, as well as flying targets. I think it's also more satisfying to learn this way because you are using what God has given you to aim and shoot the bow, without the aid of mechanical devices. You can also shoot accurately in low-light situations, when people won't be able to see their bow sights well enough to shoot. Most of all, it's fun to see how you can look at a spot and shoot an arrow to that spot without any help; it's just you and your bow and arrows."

That seemed to satisfy Luke, so he turned to the bales and, trying to follow all his uncle's instructions, loosed an arrow from five yards. It hit the bale! Luke smiled and looked at Jack for approval.

"Good job, Luke," Jack said, "with your natural athletic ability you'll get the hang of this in no time." Luke felt proud that Jack had confidence in him. "I want you to practice your form this whole week. Just practice twenty minutes a day. Then you'll be ready to shoot at specific targets. It's important that you concentrate on what you're doing, so you don't develop bad habits. Over time you'll become confident in your ability to shoot. Concentration and confidence are probably the most important parts of becoming a good archer. Now go ahead and shoot for awhile. I'll leave you alone for a few minutes." Jack purposely left Luke to practice by himself so he could concentrate without worrying about what Jack thought.

Luke felt more at ease without Jack watching, so he began shooting, paying attention to what Jack had taught him. At first the whole process seemed awkward, like anything attempted for the first time, but within a few minutes he was feeling much more comfortable. By the time Jack returned, Luke was anxious to show him the progress he had made. Luke couldn't explain it, but there was something magical about shooting an arrow, something he couldn't explain, but he knew he wanted to continue shooting.

Jack watched Luke shoot a few times, then gave him a few more pointers before Luke shot again. After a few more minutes, Jack suggested that Luke stop practicing for the day, before he got tired and developed some bad shooting habits.

"Aren't you going to shoot some more?" Luke asked, hoping Jack would say yes.

"I suppose so," Jack said, "but I'll replace this target point with what's called a judo point. This point keeps the arrow from burying itself in the ground, where you will lose it. Then we'll just take a little walk and shoot at stumps and things."

As they walked, Jack stopped and pointed to a clump of grass twenty five yards away. He quickly drew his bow and shot in one quick motion. The arrow sped through the air, easy to see because of the white feathers, and landed in the center of the clump of grass. Luke trotted over and retrieved the arrow. Jack didn't give Luke a chance to say anything before he said, "Next week, after you've practiced your form, I'll teach you how I aim." Contented with this, Luke handed the arrow to Jack and they continued on their walk, Jack casually picking out targets and shooting as they walked.

As they continued, an old piece of wood caught Luke's eye. It was a wedge that had been cut out of the tree when Al had cut the tree down after it had been struck by lightning years before. Bending over and grabbing the wedge, which was perhaps twelve inches in diameter and surprisingly light, Luke said, "I'll throw this up in the air and you shoot it."

"Okay," Jack said, "Toss it up about ten to fifteen feet." Luke obliged, tossing the piece of wood with an underhand motion. When the piece of wood reached its maximum height, the arrow was on its way and hit the wedge before it began to descend, making it fall in an erratic fashion with the arrow firmly embedded in the soft wood.

"Will I ever be able to do that?" Luke asked, amazed at Jack's skill with his bow.

Jack laughed. "Lot's of people have learned to do that sort of thing, and you can too if you practice, and follow proper form. We'd better get back to the house and spend time with Buster. I think we can take him off leash as long as we're both outside with him."

The two walked back to the house. Jack put his equipment in the camper before going into the mud room to get Buster. Buster was feeling fine today, seemingly recovered from his sedative and surgery. Jack snapped a leash onto his collar and they went back outside to familiarize Buster with the yard and give him an idea where his boundaries were. Jack had Luke take Buster's leash and they walked around the perimeter of the yard. It was a slow process because Buster was busy sniffing the whole time, totally absorbed in the smells of the farm. Jack was impressed with Buster's calmness, even when he saw farm animals for the first time.

After completing the tour of the perimeter, Jack gently removed the leash and encouraged Buster to explore on his own. Jack and Luke were both pleasantly surprised that Buster stayed fairly close to them and never tried to stray out of the yard. Several times Luke called Buster and the dog obediently responded. Each time, Luke praised Buster and petted him affectionately. Jack could see that Luke was getting attached to Buster. It was natural for this to happen, but Jack cautioned him to remember that Buster's purpose was to get Sam back, and that Buster would be in danger himself.

"Just don't get too attached," Jack warned.

"I know, Uncle Jack. Maybe there's another way to find Sam, where Buster wouldn't have to be placed in a dangerous situation like this."

"I don't know how, Luke. I've been over all the options, and I still think this is our best chance to find these guys, hopefully get

Sam back, and keep Buster from getting into serious trouble, but we will be putting him at risk. Is that okay with you?"

Luke didn't answer with words, just petted Buster more passionately, and finally nodded his head, affirming what he already knew.

"Come on Luke, let's sit on the porch and let Buster be out in the fresh air." They walked together and Jack put his arm around Luke, assuring him everything would work out well. "Sit here and I'll get us some iced tea," Jack said as he hurried into the house. Soon he emerged with two tall glasses of tea with plenty of big ice cubes crammed inside the glasses. "We need to make some purchases in the next few days and be ready to travel at a moment's notice. Do you have a sleeping bag?" Jack asked.

Luke had one, although he'd only used it a few times.

"That will work, especially in warmer weather," Jack said. "I'll make a list of all we'll need to have with us, and we'll pack it up tomorrow." They discussed the things they might need, all the while keeping an eye on Buster, who continued to be fascinated by the smells of the yard, and was methodically going over every square inch of his new home.

"We're going to need a smaller vehicle to tow behind my truck," Jack stated. "If we have to go back into a wooded area, the truck may be too big."

"Where do you think they will lead us?" Luke asked.

"I don't know, but I want to be prepared for anything."

The family car pulled into the driveway at that moment, and Buster went to greet it. The children fussed over him. Al and Martha were in the process of picking up bags of groceries from the trunk when Luke and Jack approached.

"We'll help," Jack said, with his eternal smile.

"What have you two been up to?" Al asked.

"Uncle Jack is teaching me to shoot a bow and arrow," Luke said.

"Jack, are you still shooting a bow? I thought you didn't have time for such things," Al said.

Jack just smiled, half embarrassed by the comment.

"We're also training Buster to stay in the yard," Luke said.

"It looks like he's adapted well," Martha interjected, nodding her head toward Buster, who was surrounded by the four younger Larson children, taking in all the attention with the joy and satisfaction only a dog can show.

"Come on, boys," Al said, "We got to do chores." The younger boys groaned but immediately obeyed. Soon everyone was in the house, and Jack and Luke put Buster in the mud room.

Late that evening, after chores and supper and time spent together as a family, Jack and Al sat at the dining room table. The children were all in bed, including Luke, who seemed unusually tired as the evening progressed. The two men sat together in silence for a time, both absorbed in deep thought. Martha sat in the living room sewing, wanting to leave the men alone.

"How are you, Jack? I mean how are you really?" his brother asked.

"I'm fine, Al," Jack responded. "You know me, I couldn't hide anything from you."

"Why don't you give up your line of work and settle down, get married, and raise children?" Al asked, acting more like a parent than a brother.

"I envy you this life, Al," Jack said. "You have a fine wife, wonderful children, and you're making a living off the land. It's a fine place to raise a family. I've still got a few things I want to do before I quit. I suppose 'quit' really isn't the proper word, because I'm not sure you ever really quit. It gets in your blood, and before you know it, it's your life, not just your job," Jack said thoughtfully. "This brief time with you makes me more aware of what I'm missing."

Chapter 6

Jack quickly changed the subject by asking Al to take a ride with him. Al didn't question his brother but followed him through the kitchen and into the mud room.

"Buster, you be a good boy and stay," Jack said as he opened the back door. "Let me get something before we go," Jack said as he climbed into the camper. "I want to see how good this monitor is," Jack told Al as they walked toward Jack's truck. "It should be good. I got it from a reliable source. You drive, Al, and I'll keep my attention on the monitor. Drive south to the highway and go east to the top of the hill." As they approached the crest of the hill, Jack turned on the monitor. The beam flashed brightly.

"We must be at least two miles away," Jack said, pleased so far with the performance of the tracking device. The truck continued east over the hill. The monitor still flashed, although the signal was weaker. The two men then proceeded to test the monitor to see how it performed under various circumstances. They arrived at the conclusion that the monitor would work in almost any condition up to five miles, farther than that in open country, but not much farther if there were a lot of woods or other obstacles between the transmitter and the monitor.

"I'm satisfied," Jack said finally, and Al turned the truck around and headed for home.

"Do you think Luke could be in danger if he goes along?" Al asked for at least the second time.

"I really don't think so, but if it looks like it could be, I'll have him leave and I'll possibly have to leave myself as I don't want Luke by himself any more than I have to," Jack said. "I don't think these people are so desperate that they would need to use deadly force to keep their little secret, but I never underestimate how people might behave if they are cornered or feel threatened."

"I'll leave him in your hands Jack," Al said. "I know he'll be safe with you, and I know you'll need at least one other person to help with this type of job."

Soon the truck pulled into the driveway. Both men got out. They whispered good night because the upstairs bedroom windows were open. Jack went into the camper and his brother went into the house, saying, "Hi" to Buster as he passed through the mud room.

Chapter  7

The next day Luke and his brothers had to grind feed for the cows. Luke had let Buster loose when he went out to start chores and he stayed in the yard. Buster greeted Jack at the end of the driveway as he came back from his run. Buster was fitting in well and even Jack was getting attached to him. As he knelt beside him, he praised him for being a good dog. Buster responded with a submissive tail wag and nuzzled as close to Jack as he could get.

"After all this is over, you can live here and I'll come visit you," Jack said, surprising himself that he was also enjoying Buster's company. After a shower and breakfast, he headed for Dowagiac to get supplies, as he had told Luke. Before the boys started grinding feed, Luke decided to practice with his bow. He did everything Jack told him, including staying close to the bales, even though he was tempted to move back and try longer shots. Both Gus and Jay wanted to try to shoot but neither was strong enough to draw the bow, and Luke didn't know if Jack wanted them to shoot it anyway.

Soon he was done practicing and the boys started grinding feed. They had to load the grinder with corn and mix in various ingredients to come up with the proper nutritional formula. When they were done, they moved the grinder from the corn crib to the barn and swung the auger around and through a small window in the barn, and unloaded the ground feed in the small enclosed room. This whole process took a couple of hours and lunch was ready before they finished.

Just as the family was finishing lunch Jack pulled into the yard with his pickup, towing a white Jeep Wrangler. Luke went out to see the jeep. Jack was already unhitching it from the tow bar. As Luke approached, Jack turned and said, "It's used, but it's in good shape and we can tow it behind the truck easily. Why don't we take it for a drive?" Jack got in the passenger side. Luke looked at Jack and Jack motioned him to get in the driver's seat.

"I may need you to drive this sometime," he told Luke. "Do you feel comfortable with a stick shift?" Like most farm boys, Luke had been driving tractors for years and a stick shift was all he had ever used, except for the family car.

"No problem," Luke said, confidently.

"Let's go around the block," Jack said, laughing as he gave Luke the key.

The jeep was a smaller vehicle than Luke was used to driving, but it was easy to drive and was certainly easy to maneuver. When they pulled back into the yard Jack told Luke to park the jeep close to the granery so passersby wouldn't see strange vehicles in the driveway.

"We don't want to make anything look different," Jack said. "I think we can start leaving Buster out now. He'll stay at home and it'll be good that he's visible so people can see you have a new dog. I also bought some groceries and other things, like mosquito repellent and other camping stuff, in case we have to rough it," he said, smiling at Luke. Luke was beginning to feel like he was an important part of this plan, which he really hadn't felt before.

"I practiced with the bow this morning," Luke told Jack.

Chapter 7

"How'd you do?" Jack asked. "Did you stay close to the bales?"

"Yeah, but I think I could move back a little," Luke said.

"Just stay up close and work on your form, Luke. I'll show you a couple things tomorrow when you practice again," Jack said. They got out of the jeep and walked to the house together. Luke opened the door to the mud room and called Buster. Soon Buster's head appeared at the half open screen door, as if he were testing the weather before he committed himself to coming out into the warm midday sun. When his body cleared the doorway Luke told him to stick around and then Jack and Luke went inside.

Martha had saved some lunch for Jack. He quickly washed and sat down. "I'm not used to service like this!" he exclaimed as Sandra and Nancy brought his food to the table. The girls giggled and blushed, delighted that Uncle Jack noticed and appreciated them. Martha came in with a large glass of iced tea and a pitcher for refills.

"This is great, Martha," Jack said. "You'll spoil me."

Luke kept an eye on Buster the rest of the afternoon. He was surprised at how similar Buster's habits were to Sam's. He actually lay down in Sam's favorite spot in the yard, a worn depression under the big maple tree that shaded a good portion of the front yard.

Late that evening Luke asked Jack how he would know if the dog thieves knew about Buster.

"We may not know until they take him, Luke," Jack replied. "We don't want to spend a lot of time looking for someone unusual to stop in or drive by. If we act suspicious, they won't take Buster, and our plan will fail. I suspect they'll be here on Sunday, like before if they feel they're safe in repeating their crime."

Luke was beginning to get excited, not only at the prospect of saving Sam. He was about to go on an adventure, something different than the day-to-day life of a farm boy. Luke fidgeted for a while before approaching Jack with another question. "Could I borrow your cell phone, Uncle Jack?" he finally asked. "I need to call someone, and if I use our phone, everyone can hear me."

Jack smiled. "Sure," he said, reaching into his pocket and handing it to Luke. After a few simple instructions, Luke went out to the mud room to make his call to Sue, who he hadn't talked with in a few days. He wanted to explain that he might be gone for several days and he wouldn't be able to ask her out for Saturday night. Sue seemed disappointed, but still seemed friendly. Luke still wondered if she really liked him, as he wasn't able to take her out as often as most of the boys in school. He promised he would call as soon as he got back. She asked where he was going and all he told her was that he was going on a short trip with his Uncle Jack, and he didn't know for sure where they would end up. He hated to end the conversation but Luke knew that cell phone calls could be expensive so he said he had to go.

After hanging up, Luke realized that for the first time he really had feelings for a girl, but with those feelings came so many questions, and fears of her not liking him, and all the things associated with the beginning of a relationship. Luke seemed a little overwhelmed by these newfound emotions. He took the phone back to Jack. "Thanks, Uncle Jack," he said as he handed over the phone. "I think I'll go to bed. I don't feel so good. I think I'm just tired."

"Go ahead," Jack answered. "I'll check on Buster before I go to bed."

Soon everybody was on their way to bed. All the lights were out as Jack walked out to check on Buster before entering the camper. He could see Buster resting in his bed under the maple tree, attentive to the night sounds and aware of Jack's presence. Jack quickly went to the camper so Buster didn't feel the need to get up. As he started to open the door he heard a vehicle coming slowly down the road from the south. It was going a little too slow, Jack thought, as he crept into the shadows on the far side of the house. He could see the truck coming down the road, so slowly that Buster got up to sniff the air, although he did not bark. As the truck passed in front of the house a spot light appeared through the passenger side window and focused on Buster. Buster barked once and walked toward the truck, which maintained its slow pace for a few more seconds. The spot light went off and the truck resumed normal speed as it headed north.

Jack knew that things were going to happen soon. He felt the exhilaration that comes from completing a task you set out to accomplish. Of course, this was only the first step, but he knew these people would be back for Buster—soon!

Jack had never been a sound sleeper. It wasn't a part of his nature, and now that he knew things were falling into place he didn't want to lose any advantage he might have, so he slept as he often slept while on the job, a half-sleep not unlike that of wild animals. He finally got up at about 5:15 and was reading his Bible when he heard the back door of the house open. Jack opened his camper door and saw Luke sitting on the cement step outside the mud room, putting on his boots and petting Buster, who had come to greet him.

"You're up early," Jack said in a matter-of-fact voice.

"Yeah, I went to bed early and just couldn't sleep anymore," Luke responded, but he seemed cheerful and pleasant.

"Are your mom and dad up yet?" Jack asked.

"Yeah, Mom just put some coffee on," Luke said.

"Take your boots off and come in the house for a minute so I can talk to you and your folks," Jack said in a serious tone that made Luke realize something important was happening. Inside, Martha handed Jack a cup of coffee and the four of them sat down at the kitchen table while Jack related the events of the previous night.

"When do you think they'll be back?" Al asked.

"My guess will be Sunday, while everyone's at church. It worked for them before and it's about the only time when no one is around here," Jack said. "It's important we don't act any different or do anything out of the ordinary between now and then."

Luke could feel his heart quicken as he began to get excited. He could sense that he was about to embark on an adventure, something he couldn't even imagine based on his limited experience outside of farm life.

"I've got to pick up a few groceries to put in the camper, and I think I'm ready to go," Jack said.

"Do you have any idea how long you'll be gone?" Martha asked with motherly concern in her voice.

"It's hard to say," Jack answered. "We know they're transporting the dogs to some place where there is privacy and they don't have to worry about noise that dogs might make, and have people snooping around. We'll just have to follow them and see where they lead us. Once there, we'll contact the local authorities and our job will be done."

Satisfied with Jack's answer, Martha turned to Luke and asked if he was all packed. Luke had his sleeping bag but really hadn't thought about what else he should take with him.

"Just pack a few changes of clothes and personal stuff like a tooth brush," Jack said. "I don't have a lot of room in my camper, so we'll have to travel light. We'll get ready to go Saturday evening and figure out if we need anything else then."

Luke went out to do his chores and left the three adults alone to discuss the details of the trip.

After breakfast Luke took the bow out to practice before it got hot and before he got involved in work around the farm. Jack watched from his camper as Luke shot several arrows into the bales from close range. Satisfied with Luke's progress, Jack went over to give him further instructions.

"You're learning to shoot very quickly, Luke," Jack said. "I think it's time I showed you how to aim the bow. I don't even know if aiming is the right word, but it gets the point across."

Chapter 7

Luke handed Jack the bow, anxious to see what Jack was going to teach him.

"There are different ways to shoot the bow and be accurate, Luke," Jack began. "I'll show you what worked for me. Once you become more experienced you will probably find a method that works best for you. I shoot with all three fingers under the arrow. I anchor high on my cheek so my eye is close to the arrow. I don't really look down the arrow but actually concentrate on my target. My brain recognizes the gap between the tip of the arrow and the spot I want to hit, and through practice, my subconscious tells me where to point the arrow in relation to the target.

"The most important thing to remember is, once you consciously look down the arrow at the target to see the gap between the tip of the arrow and the target, you must focus on the target exclusively as you shoot. With practice you won't even consciously look down the arrow at all. You'll just pick a spot you want the arrow to hit, and you automatically raise or lower the bow so you can hit the target. The secret is to start close and gradually work your way to further distances."

Jack then gave the bow back to Luke and helped him with his first aiming lesson. He had Luke keep his bow arm straight and solid. Then he helped him establish an anchor point, a spot that he drew the arrow back to consistently every time. Then he taught Luke to totally concentrate on the spot he wanted the arrow to hit, and finally discussed releasing the arrow. Within thirty minutes Luke was able to place his arrow consistently within a couple of inches of his intended target at thirty feet. It excited Luke greatly to think he could, just by looking at a spot, send an arrow there without mechanical sights or aids of any sort. He tried to explain his feelings to Jack, but really couldn't describe what he felt.

Jack smiled. "That's why I still shoot the bow," he said. "It's one of the great joys of my life." There was awkward silence before Jack told Luke he'd better put the bow away before he over practiced and developed some bad habits.

Luke walked with Jack back to the camper and put the bow away. "I'm going to go into town and pick up a few things," Jack said as he put the bow in a closet. This evening we'll get most of your stuff packed in here and be ready to go."

"Uncle Jack," Luke said after a moment's silence. "Thanks for all you are doing for me. I don't know how we would get Sam without you. And thanks for spending time with me," Luke concluded, feeling awkward at what he had just said.

"I've enjoyed it, Luke," Jack said, sensing Luke's awkwardness. "It's been fun finding Buster, and it's been fun spending time with you and your family. Now you'd better spend some time with Buster and I'll go to town and be back here later this afternoon. Say, tomorrow's Saturday. Don't you have another date?" Jack teased.

Luke shifted uneasily. "I wanted to, but I didn't want to be gone from home and have Buster stolen, and you might need to follow them without me."

"That's probably good thinking," Jack said, becoming more serious. "Tonight I'll show you how to read the tracking device and you'll be able to handle the monitor." The two left the camper, Luke going to spend time with Buster as Jack headed for his truck to go to town.

Buster seemed happy as Luke approached. He was the type of dog who didn't feel that he needed to be around people constantly. He was content to be by himself, as long as his new family acknowledged him occasionally. Buster was also beginning to take his new job as "watch dog" seriously, as it was his instinct to protect.

Soon Al came outside and told Luke what had to be done around the farm today. Together they started on the tasks, the first of which was repairing the woven wire fence in the barn yard. Gus and Jay had to clean up the milking parlor and entryway from the barn yard into the barn. The day seemed to go quickly, and soon it was chore time again.

Jack came back just as the evening milking was finished. The whole family ate together, including Jack. Martha had made meat loaf, with lots of potatoes and carrots, and apple pie for dessert. After supper Jack and Luke went to the camper where they worked on the tracking device. They then took a ride so Jack could show Luke how to use the device while they were moving. The monitor was simple to read so it didn't take Luke long to learn what he needed to know. Jack encouraged Luke to relax and go to bed early as he needed to be well rested when the time came to follow these people.

Jack was dozing off later that night when he heard the slow-moving truck coming along the road in front of the house. He slipped out of the camper, in bare feet, and cautiously peered around the corner of the house as the truck slowly came closer. Buster was already standing, looking in the direction of the truck, the hair on the middle of his back raised, as if he knew this vehicle was up to no good. Jack could even hear him growl softly as the truck came in line with the driveway. Just like the previous night, a spot light suddenly came on and pointed at Buster as the truck continued its slow path to the north. As the truck passed, Jack ran to the other corner of the house to see if he could observe anything else. The spot light was off by the time he got to the other side of the house but the truck continued to drive slowly, perhaps picking up a little speed as it got closer to the creek.

Jack felt that everything was in place, and these guys would be back soon, probably Sunday. Confident that he had prepared the best he could, he walked back to the camper and soon was sleeping as soundly as his mind would allow. Buster had resumed his position under the maple tree and once again relaxed, as much as a working dog can relax.

Chapter  8

Saturday morning started much like every other day on the farm. Luke was awake early, filled with excitement and anticipation. He again was first out of the house but Jack was already up and doing some sort of stretching exercises beside the camper. Buster was sitting a few feet away watching Jack with his head cocked and ears raised, as if he were questioning Jack's reason for doing these strange things.

"Hi, Uncle Jack," Luke said. "It looks like Buster is coaching you, making sure you do it right."

Jack laughed as he stood up. "I believe he thinks I'm crazy," he said. Then he got more serious. "I saw the truck drive by again last night. You'd better stay home from church tomorrow so we'll be ready to go if they come for Buster."

"They make me mad because they're so bold," Luke said with obvious annoyance.

Jack cautioned him not to get upset. "Always keep a cool head, son. You think better and react better when you're not upset."

Luke didn't answer, just headed out to the barn to get his chores started.

After breakfast Luke went out with Jack and they shot their bows together, with Jack giving Luke further instructions. "If you don't remember anything else, Luke, remember this: Once you get the mechanics of shooting down, confidence and concentration are the most important aspects of shooting well."

Before the session ended Luke was shooting from fifteen yards and was quite consistent, as long as he concentrated on the very center of the spot he wished to hit with his arrow.

"You're a good student and a fast learner," Jack said as they went to retrieve Luke's arrows. "Nock an arrow, Luke," Jack said. He took a small rubber ball out of his pocket and showed it to Luke. "I'm going to stand off to your right and roll the ball to your left. Concentrate on the ball and try to hit it," Jack ordered. Luke positioned himself as Jack walked several steps away. He then rolled the ball. Luke raised his bow instinctively, followed the ball, and shot. He didn't hit the ball, but he came within a foot or so, which wasn't bad, according to Jack. They did this a few more times and Luke got closer, but didn't hit the ball.

"We'd better put the bows up now, before you develop some bad habits," Jack said. "You're doing better than I ever expected so soon."

Luke truly enjoyed shooting the bow. When he shot, he concentrated so much on the act of shooting that he literally forgot about everything else. Jack interrupted his thoughts by reminding him that they would go deer hunting with the bows this fall. "You'll enjoy the challenge," he told Luke. After they put the bows into the camper, Jack told Luke to get all his stuff out to the camper so he could pack it. When Luke came out of the house with his two duffle bags, Jack was backing up the truck under the camper. Within fifteen minutes the camper was loaded on the truck.

"It's best to keep the truck and camper right here, where it can't be easily seen. It'll only take a minute to hook the jeep behind the truck, so we'll leave it unhitched for now."

Chapter 8

That evening Martha made a special supper of roast beef with mashed potatoes and gravy and green peas, Luke's favorite meal of all time. Everyone ate until they were stuffed, including Jack, who usually only ate small portions.

"Now for a surprise," Martha said. She disappeared into the kitchen and came out with a large carrot cake that said, "Happy Birthday, Jack."

Jack was visibly surprised and a little embarrassed. "It's not my birthday," he finally said, in his defense.

"It's close enough," Martha said. "Al told me carrot cake is your favorite. Is that true?"

"Yes, he's right about that, but I didn't save much room for cake," Jack said. Al lit several candles and the family sang "Happy Birthday." Jack couldn't remember when he had felt this close to his family, probably not since his high school days. He made the first cut but then insisted that Martha do the rest of the cutting. Everyone laughed and talked and had a good time. The four smaller children obviously loved their Uncle Jack and the feeling was mutual. Later in the evening as the girls were cleaning up the table, Jack thanked everybody.

"This is the best birthday I can remember," he said. "Thanks, everybody."

Just before dark Luke went to check on Buster, who was in his spot under the maple tree. He wagged his tail and sat up as Luke approached. Luke got down on his knees and petted Buster, vigorously at first and then slowly, all the while talking to him about how good a dog he was and that he wasn't going to let anything happen to him. Luke didn't think Buster understood, but it made him feel better to tell Buster. Then he said good night and went in the house.

The four younger children were already upstairs in bed and the three adults were sitting around the dining room table, drinking coffee. Jack was facing Luke as he entered the dining room. He motioned for Luke to sit down by him, then began to tell Al and Martha that the dog thieves would probably come tomorrow.

"I need you to leave for church just the same as usual. If they come and take Buster, we'll load up the jeep and be hot on their trail. We'll have my cell phone so we can communicate and keep you posted on where we are. We've got adequate food and supplies for several days, although this shouldn't take very long. I wouldn't think their camp would be too far away; otherwise, they wouldn't be back in this area so soon after stealing Sam. We'll stay out of harm's way, and when we find their camp I'll use the cell phone to call the local authorities. Then we'll be on our way home with Sam and Buster," Jack concluded.

"Promise me you'll be careful, both of you," Martha said, with a very serious look on her face.

"We'll be careful, Martha," Jack promised. All this talk made Luke even more excited, and he knew he wasn't going to sleep much, because he wasn't even tired.

"We'd all better get to bed," Al finally said. Luke went upstairs and got undressed, but he heard his dad talking to Uncle Jack. He couldn't help but try to eavesdrop. He silently kneeled next to the heat register and looked down at the two men sitting at the table. Jack was talking.

"I think I've covered all the angles, Al, and if we have any surprises, or it begins to look dangerous, we'll back off and let the local authorities do their job. I won't jeopardize Luke's well-being for Sam or Buster. He's more important then they are." Al agreed. Luke then got up and crawled into bed. He didn't feel more important than his dogs, but he knew that if he said anything like that, his parents wouldn't let him go.

Soon he heard Jack say good night as he went to the camper and his parents came upstairs. Luke lay still for what seemed like an hour before he drifted off into a fitful sleep, with dreams of Sam, Buster and himself, saving them and bringing them safely home. He woke several times but managed to go back to sleep.

Chapter  9

At 5:30 Al was standing by Luke's bed, surprised that he wasn't up already.

"I guess I didn't sleep much," Luke told his dad as he stretched, sat up, scratched his head, and tried to part his hair. Jay and Gus were still sleeping, and Al said he was going to let them sleep.

"Jack's going to help me milk," Al said. "Let's get started." He started downstairs. Luke's heart was already beating fast, anticipating what the next few hours might bring. He knew he was ready to go get his Sam.

It seemed a little strange to Luke that Uncle Jack was doing chores but since Jack also had grown up on a farm it wasn't foreign to him and it wasn't long before the chores were done. Luke tried to do some things ahead so his chores wouldn't be as hard for Jay and Gus to do while he was gone. When the three went up to the house, the children were already done bathing and eating, and were getting ready for church. The smell of frying bacon filled the house.

"Hi, Mom," Luke said, as he gave Martha a hug while she continued to face the stove and work. She smiled and turned to acknowledge his affection, but had both hands busy. Martha was tall as women go, but Luke was already taller than her by a good three inches. In fact, Luke was almost as tall as his dad.

Luke quickly washed and sat down at the kitchen table to eat. He felt exceptionally hungry this morning, even though he was excited. Al and Jack seemed hungry too, and they all ate several pancakes apiece. Martha even had to make more batter to finish feeding the men. As Al finished the last bite of his last pancake, Martha refilled all the coffee cups and sat down herself, which was unusual. Jack and Al must have also thought it strange to have Martha sit down at the kitchen table on a Sunday morning because they both stopped talking and looked at her.

Realizing she was being stared at, she asked, "Can't a woman sit down and be with her family at breakfast?" Everyone laughed, but Luke could tell that his mom was uneasy about his going with Jack.

Soon she turned to him. "I want you to do everything your Uncle Jack tells you, and use good judgment. I packed a little lunch for both of you. If these people don't come, you'll have to eat it anyway." She attempted to smile but it was a nervous smile that quickly faded. This was the first time Luke would be away from home, and her mothering instincts kept telling her that he might be in danger, although she tried not to think that way.

Jack must have sensed her concern, because he told her his plans again, and promised to use the cell phone to keep in touch. Martha knew that, and tried to shrug off her feelings, but still felt uneasy about the whole thing. She got up from the table, gathered the dishes and put them in the sink.

Nancy and Sandra came into the kitchen and started washing the dishes. Jay and Gus could be heard in the other room arguing about something. Al remained seated at the table but called out to them. "It seems like you boys get along better when you have to do chores in the morning. Not enough time to argue, I guess." He and Jack both smiled as it got very quiet in the next room. "They obviously like the idea of not doing chores in the morning!" Al said quietly. Everyone smiled as they got up from the table to get ready for church. Jack went out to the camper.

Luke took a shower and dressed in Levis and a blue T-shirt. When he came downstairs obviously not dressed for church, the other children protested, all wanting to stay home and go with Jack.

"We've been over this before," Martha scolded. "Now say good-bye to Luke and get out to the car." The two girls gave Luke a hug and went to the car. The two boys just said, "Bye" and shuffled off to the car, still not happy that Luke got to go someplace without them.

Finally Al came downstairs, wearing the same dark blue sport coat he had worn for as long as Luke could remember. He extended his hand to Luke but then decided to hug him instead. "You're getting so big I don't know how to treat you," he told Luke as they embraced. "Be careful and do what your uncle tells you."

"I will, Dad," Luke said, looking into his father's eyes. Al looked at Luke only briefly before looking away. Luke thought he might be crying, but couldn't tell for sure.

Then Martha gave him a big hug that lasted several seconds, but she didn't say anything. She just looked up at Luke, her eyes watering, and then turned and quickly hugged Jack. Then they quickly left the house, slightly embarrassed about the display of emotion.

Luke watched through the window as they drove down the driveway and turned south onto the gravel road. Luke felt kind of strange as his family left, probably because they had made such a big deal about his going away. Jack watched Luke as he followed the car from window to window until it was out of sight.

"It's nice to know you're loved," Jack finally said. Luke didn't know how to respond and finally said, "Yeah," just to acknowledge Jack's statement.

"We'd better stay away from the windows now, Luke," Jack continued. "Where can we get the best view of the driveway and yard?"

"Probably from my bedroom," Luke said, leading the way. It wasn't long before they heard a truck come down the road and pull into the driveway. They peered through the window without moving the curtains.

"Oh, no," Jack said. "It's the milk truck." Every two days the milk truck came to take the milk that was stored in the milk tank. Although this was a normal event, it might change the thieves' plans, Jack thought.

"It only takes a few minutes to load the milk onto the truck," Luke explained. "They'll be gone in no time." The two could only sit on the beds and wait, the sun filtering through the windows in a way that revealed all the fine dust particles floating effortlessly through the air.

Soon the truck pulled out of the driveway and all was quiet. Buster had got up from his bed beneath the maple tree to investigate the milk truck but quickly resumed his post when it left. Several minutes passed in silence. Jack was absorbed in thought and Luke was so anxious he could hardly stand it. Jack sensed Luke's anxiety and placed a hand on his shoulder.

"Relax," he said as he squeezed Luke's shoulder. "Sometimes the hardest thing to do is wait," he said with a smile.

Luke wondered how Jack could be so composed. He was about to say something when he heard the sound of a truck coming down the road. Jack was already looking out the window. Luke joined him as an older, light red pickup truck pulled into the driveway. A big wooden box sat in the bed of the pickup.

Chapter 9

"Don't touch the curtains," Jack cautioned Luke, "and try not to get upset about what happens next." Buster was already on his way to the truck to investigate. The driver's side window slowly lowered and the barrel of a gun appeared. Buster stopped and growled. He had cautiously started to circle the truck when Luke heard what he thought was a shot. Suddenly Buster was spinning around, biting at his right hip area. Buster instinctively backed away from the truck but then began to circle it again.

"They shot him with the tranquilizer gun," Jack explained. "Usually it takes five to ten minutes to take effect." Luke didn't reply. He had a hard time remaining quiet and inactive when Buster was in trouble, but he reminded himself that this is what had to be done to stop these people, and especially to find Sam.

After cautiously circling the truck, Buster stopped to lick his hip area for several seconds. Then he slowly walked back to the maple tree and laid down. "They're waiting for Buster to fall asleep before they get him," Jack explained. Luke didn't respond, but the thought of these people coming into his yard and shooting his dog upset him greatly. He started shaking uncontrollably, like the time he had got real cold a few winters ago riding back home on the tractor after helping his Dad cut wood. Jack put his arm around Luke as they stood side by side, waiting for the next move.

Minutes passed before the passenger door slowly opened. A big man wearing a ball cap got out and cautiously walked to the front of the truck. Buster didn't move but the man remained still. He wore a plaid, long-sleeved shirt, sleeves rolled up to the elbows. The shirt was unbuttoned, exposing a dirty white T-shirt. He slowly walked closer to Buster. Buster continued to lie in his bed beneath the maple tree, on his side and panting, as the stranger approached. The man was now within a few feet of Buster. He had broken a small branch from an overhanging limb on the maple tree and proceeded to poke Buster, who failed to respond.

Confident, the huge stranger picked up Buster behind the front legs, and once he got him up, put his right arm under his abdomen and proceeded to carry Buster back to the truck. The driver got out and put down the tail gate. He then raised the front of the box and waited for his companion to place Buster in the box. Once this was accomplished, the driver let the door slide back down. The door had two holes in it, each about three inches in diameter. Each man looked through the holes briefly. Apparently satisfied, they put up the tail gate, got in the truck, and slowly backed out of the driveway. Once on the gravel road, they slowly proceeded north.

Jack and Luke moved to the girls' bedroom so they could make sure the truck continued north until the truck passed between the bushes and trees that lined the creek.

"Let's go," Jack said. Luke instinctively moved for the stairs, Jack leading. "I'll pull the truck around into the driveway. Bring the jeep right up behind the truck."

Luke ran to get the jeep. It started right up. He noticed it had a full tank of gas. By the time he had turned the jeep around Jack was parked in the driveway, and was standing behind the truck, ready to guide Luke closer so they could attach the jeep to the truck. Jack guided Luke with hand signals until he was satisfied, which he signified by raising both hands, fingers spread and palms facing Luke. Luke stopped the jeep, put it in neutral, and got out.

Jack lowered the tow bar from the front of the jeep and attempted to attach it to the hitch ball, which was attached to the back of the truck. Luke could see the tow bar wasn't close enough so he pulled the jeep a couple of inches closer to the truck until Jack was able to attach the tow bar to the receiver. He then quickly attached two chains from the jeep to the truck so the two vehicles wouldn't separate even if the tow bar failed. Then Jack opened the hood and took out a wire, which he plugged into another wire by the license plate of the truck. This wire would make the rear lights of the jeep go on when the truck brakes were applied. Quickly,

Chapter 9

Jack checked the hookups, and, satisfied, motioned for Luke to get in the truck.

Once in the truck, Jack turned on the tracking device. The signal was strong and the blinking green light showed that the dog thieves were slowly heading north. Jack turned north out of the driveway, periodically checking the jeep through his rearview mirrors. Luke was beginning to regain his composure. Being able to do something physical was helpful and made him feel like he was contributing.

"We want to stay out of the sight of those two," Jack said as he increased his speed. "If I stay a half mile behind them that will work." Jack and Luke continued to follow the pickup by way of the tracking device as it continued north, until they got on I-94. They proceeded east toward Kalamazoo, and then turned north on US 131. "They're definitely heading north," Jack said. "How far north is anybody's guess. Reach behind your seat and see if you can find the atlas of county maps."

Luke was quiet, fearful that asking too many questions might irritate Jack, although Jack never acted irritated by anything Luke said.

"How are you feeling?" Jack finally asked, sensing Luke's concerns.

"I'm okay," Luke answered. "Is it better for us that they are heading north?"

Jack was beginning to be concerned about gas for the truck when the signal on the monitor became stationary.

"They stopped," Luke exclaimed.

"They probably need to get gas, too," Jack said. "I think we're coming into Kalkaska. I'll stop at the first station and fill up so we'll be ready to go." They pulled into a station on the outskirts of Kalkaska and quickly filled up.

"You want a bottle of pop?" Jack asked as he went inside to pay.

"Get a coke for me, please," Luke answered.

When Jack returned and started the truck he looked at the monitor. The pickup they were following hadn't moved, according to the signal.

"Let's see what's going on," Jack said as he pulled onto the highway. They had gone only a quarter of a mile when they both spotted the dull red truck parked in front of a bar. Several other cars were also parked in front of the bar, an obviously popular spot for the locals. Jack pulled into a parking lot for a party store across the road. The two sat for a few minutes before Jack decided to go into the bar.

"You stay here," Luke. "I'm going inside to see if I can get an idea about where they're going. Maybe I won't find out anything, but I'll get up close to these guys so I can size them up." Luke didn't know what Jack meant by that, but he wasn't about to ask. "I'll bring a hamburger back for you," Jack said as he closed the door. Luke was getting hungry. It was close to seven o'clock according to his watch and they'd already eaten the lunch his mom had packed. Jack crossed the road and entered the bar without looking back.

After a few moments Luke got the idea that he could walk across the road and look inside the box on the bed of the red pickup and see if Buster was okay. He thought about the benefits of such an action. The disadvantages were numerous, the worst being that he might get caught, ruining everything, so he decided it wasn't worth doing. He would just sit in the truck and wait for Jack.

Inside the bar, Jack seated himself at a table close to the two dog thieves, who were sitting on bar stools eating and also drinking quite a lot of beer. They didn't really draw attention to themselves but Jack could hear most everything they said. The smaller man, who was doing the driving, was quite thin, with three or four days' growth of whiskers on his face. He wore a green cap with a

John Deere logo on the front. The bigger thief was so large he looked out of place sitting on the bar stool. He wasn't really fat, just big and burly and his rolled-up shirt sleeves revealed thick, muscular forearms.

He turned to the smaller man. "What time is Dorsey expecting us?"

The thin man looked at his watch. "Any time before midnight, I guess. He should be happy with this one. He's young, strong and only needs a little training. We'll have to see how tough he is when we get to camp." Their talk then drifted to other things and the waitress brought Jack's take-out order so he got up and went back to his truck.

"Did you find out anything?" Luke asked even before Jack was able to get in the truck.

"We've still got three or four hours' ride ahead of us, which means we're either going to the Upper Peninsula or into Canada. I hope we stay in the United States, simply because I don't know my way around Canada as well and I don't know how much help the local authorities will be with us being the foreigners. The one guy looks as strong as an ox, and almost as big. That's really all I could tell. Let's eat our burgers before they get cold. I also got us fries and a couple of cokes."

The two ate in silence as they waited for the two men inside the bar to come out and resume their trip. Just as they were finishing the two thieves stepped out of the bar. The driver walked behind the truck to look through one of the air holes. He backed up suddenly, which probably meant Buster was awake and on the defensive. The thin man got into the driver's seat. The bigger man was already in the truck. Once again they headed north.

Jack waited a minute or so before starting his truck and resuming their journey. Luke kept wishing he had gone to see Buster, and finally told Jack his thoughts and his reasons for not doing it.

"You were smart not to. It could have put the whole operation in jeopardy. You made the right choice, Luke. That's good!" Jack kept his eyes on the road. They followed the truck through Petosky and continued north toward the tip of the Lower Peninsula of Michigan. "We'll soon see if they're heading for Canada," Jack said. "The Mackinaw Bridge is just a few miles ahead. If they head toward Sault Saint Marie they're probably going for the Canadian border."

Luke looked up ahead through the gathering dusk. He could see a lot of lights. He hadn't seen the bridge linking the Upper and Lower Peninsulas before, although he'd seen pictures and even watched a documentary on the building of the bridge. As they entered I-75 and went through Mackinaw City the bridge ahead looked long and more beautiful than Luke had envisioned.

"I'm going to get closer to their truck so we can keep an eye on them," Jack explained as he increased his speed.

"There they are," Luke said as he pointed ahead. The dull red truck was perhaps four hundred yards ahead of them and already over the water of Lakes Michigan and Huron. Luke couldn't help but look down at the blue water with occasional white-capped waves. He looked to the west and saw the sun low on the horizon. Then Luke looked up to see how high the cables went, and could barely see the top because the front of the camper blocked his vision.

"This bridge is something, isn't it?" Jack asked as they passed the halfway point of the bridge.

"I didn't know it was this big, and we're higher above the water than I thought," Luke exclaimed.

"You aren't afraid of heights, are you?" Jack joked.

Soon the toll booths came into sight. Jack was careful to not get in line right behind the red truck, as several booths were open. They were shortly on their way again, but soon the red truck's right turn signal came on and they turned onto U.S. 2 and headed west out of St. Ignace, the town on the Upper Peninsula side of the bridge.

"It looks like we're staying in the U.P., Luke. If these boys were going to Wisconsin, they probably would have driven through Chicago and headed north. That's a bit of a relief," Jack said, relaxing his grip on the wheel slightly. "Let's enjoy this beautiful sunset," Jack said.

It truly was magnificent to watch as they drove west along Lake Michigan. The reddish glow of the sun on the horizon and the light reflecting off the water made for a spectacular setting. Luke was beginning to relax a little, but Jack always looked relaxed and calm. Luke thought that it was probably because Jack was relaxed that he felt he could relax, but he also was eagerly anticipating finding where they were taking Buster.

The sun was below the horizon and Jack had just turned on his headlights when the monitor showed that the red truck had once again turned north.

"We're getting close now," Jack said as he reached behind his seat and pulled out a road atlas and handed it to Luke. "Open it to the map of Michigan and see what county we're in." He once again put his arm behind the seats, blindly feeling for something, finally bringing forward another atlas. "This is a map of all the counties in Michigan. It lists most roads and even most 'two-tracks' in each county," Jack explained as he handed it to Luke. Jack handed Luke a small flashlight so he could see without using the dome light.

"There isn't much traffic now," Luke commented as they continued northward.

"No, most people have probably found a motel or a camping spot by now. There were a lot of RVs on the road today. People probably anxious to get away early in the summer," Jack said.

Luke, having never been away from the farm, was amazed that people could just leave home for extended periods of time. He felt uneasy just knowing he had missed his chores that evening. Luke's mind was wandering as he glanced at the monitor and noticed they had again changed direction.

"They're heading west again," Luke said as he looked at the map more carefully. "They probably turned left on M-28 at Seney."

"Maybe they're heading for Munising, or Marquette," Jack thought aloud. The two vehicles headed west for several miles, Jack always making sure he stayed out of sight of the truck he was following.

"They turned north again," Luke said, sensing that they must be getting close now.

Jack slowed the truck as they tried to figure out where to turn. "Thank goodness there aren't many options," Jack said as he turned north onto a county road. "There's a sign that says there's a state forest campground up ahead. We'd better pull in there quickly and park the camper and unhitch the jeep. Once we find out where they're staying we can come back to the camper."

"If we stop, we might lose them, won't we?" Luke asked.

"They're traveling slow," Jack explained, probably because the gravel road's a little rough. It won't take long to make the switch. There's a primitive campground up ahead to the left."

Jack pulled the rig into the campground. There were very few people there, mostly tent campers. He pulled into a camping space and the two quickly got out to unhook the jeep. As Jack took the hitch off and started on the chains, he told Luke to get the flashlights, maps, and monitor from the truck. When Luke returned, Jack had finished unhooking the jeep and the two jumped in. It started right away and they were once again on their way.

Luke looked at the monitor signal. It had faded but was still present. It felt funny to go from Jack's big, one-ton pickup to a Jeep Wrangler but Luke could see that the smaller vehicle could move faster on these back roads. He began studying the county maps to see where they were exactly. After a few minutes he figured that they had just left Schoolcraft County and were now in Alger County.

"Try to figure out where we are exactly and look at what roads up ahead they could turn on," Jack said.

"The signal's getting stronger again," Luke said, relieved that they hadn't lost the red truck and Buster. "It looks like they just turned onto a road heading northwest."

Jack slowed the jeep as the two looked for the road. "There it is," they both said as the headlights revealed a smaller gravel road.

Jack slowed the jeep down, fearing he might overtake the thieves and make them suspicious. "Look on the map and see what's up ahead," Jack said as he concentrated on the more bumpy road.

Even before Luke could tell exactly what roads lay ahead the signal changed direction to the north again. "They turned right up ahead somewhere," Luke informed Jack. As they approached the small path the truck had turned on Jack could suddenly feel the jeep steering with more difficulty, pulling to the left.

"Oh, no," he said as he pulled to a stop. "We've got a flat tire."

Chapter 10

Luke's heart sank. "What'll we do?" Luke asked, feeling hopeless after coming so far.

"Let's fix the flat," Jack said in a matter-of-fact tone. "The road they turned on is not even maintained by the county, and we're awful close to Pictured Rocks Natural Park, so they can't go very far," Jack said as he quickly surveyed the map of Alger County.

Both men quickly got out of the jeep and lifted the hood to get the wrench and jack. Jack handed Luke the wrench to loosen the nuts while he put the jack into the proper position under the axle of the left rear wheel. Jack got the spare tire from its place on the rear of the jeep and bounced it on the ground twice to make sure it had air in it. Satisfied, he laid the tire beside Luke, who was on his knees taking the last of the lug nuts off the wheel. Luke handed the wrench to Jack to attach to the extension on the jack so he could lift the jeep.

"Go look at the monitor," Jack ordered Luke. "See if they're still traveling."

Luke went to the passenger seat and grabbed the monitor. He looked at the green signal for almost a minute before placing it back on the seat. "Uncle Jack, the monitor is steady and not moving. They're probably one and a half to two miles northwest of us."

Jack didn't say anything at first. As Luke came around the jeep, Jack said, "That's good, because this jack doesn't work."

Luke's heart sank. "What can we do, Uncle Jack? There's no tree branches big enough to use for a lever, and I don't see any rocks to put under the jeep."

Luke was beginning to panic, and Jack knew he had to calm him. "Those two are probably in their camp now, so they aren't likely to go anywhere," Jack explained. "We've got to get this jeep out of here before they get suspicious. Then we can park it down by the road and we'll walk in and have a look at the camp." The calmness in Uncle Jack's voice had the desired effect on Luke, as he sensed that Jack was in control.

Jack continued, "I'm going to get my gloves out of the jeep. You get ready to take the tire off and put the spare on." Jack walked around the jeep to fetch his gloves while Luke dutifully readied himself to change the flat, still not knowing what Uncle Jack had in mind. Luke was still bent down by the flat tire when Jack asked if he was ready.

"Yeah, I guess," Luke said in a questioning voice. Suddenly the back end of the jeep raised up about six inches. Luke was amazed, but quickly removed the flat and put the spare on.

"Tighten the nuts as far as you can by hand," Jack said as he stood behind the jeep.

Luke quickly accomplished this task, and looked around the left rear bumper to tell Jack he was done. What he saw was hard to believe. Jack was standing behind the jeep, holding the jeep with his arms extended down by his lower thighs. "I - I - I'm done," Luke finally blurted out. Jack slowly lowered the jeep to the ground.

"Now tighten the nuts the best you can," Jack ordered, as if nothing had happened. Luke quickly tightened each nut but couldn't get the picture of Jack lifting the jeep out of his mind. When he finished Jack had already put the flat in the back of the jeep. "Put the wrench back here for tonight," Jack told Luke as he headed for the driver's seat. Luke also got into the jeep and the two slowly drove up the road.

"Here's a good spot to turn in," Jack said as he pulled the jeep off the road and about thirty feet into the woods. "I don't think they'll be able to see the jeep here if they come back out. I'll give you a set of keys. Keep them and don't lose them. Bring the mosquito repellent and let's get going." The mosquitoes had been pesky while they were changing the tire, but Luke and Jack had been busy. Now the little critters seemed worse, probably because the men were not as active.

They walked back to the two-track that the truck had used to drive into the woods. Jack told Luke to stay off the two-track to avoid making tracks in the sandy soil. They walked on the left side of the two-track, in the woods, so as not to be detected. As they walked Luke sprayed some repellent on his hands and slapped it on his neck and face. Then he sprayed the repellent on his hat, making sure his ears were protected. Then he handed the bottle to Jack, who quickly applied the repellent and handed it back to Luke.

They walked for about a mile or so through the rolling terrain before they came to a steeper hill. Jack motioned for Luke to stop and they listened in silence. There was a slight north breeze coming from Lake Superior and it had a cooling effect, which Luke welcomed. Just as he was about to ask Jack what he had heard, Luke thought he heard a dog bark.

"Let's get to the top of this hill and then go slow. We're getting close." As they came over the crest of the hill they could see lights about a quarter of a mile away. There was also the sound of a motor, probably a generator, Luke thought.

"Stay behind me from here on," Jack whispered. "They may have some devices for detecting us, although I doubt it." Flashlights were not necessary as a big full moon hung in the sky, although passing clouds would sometimes cause it to become darker.

Jack walked more slowly as they closed to within two hundred yards of the lights. Luke could hear the muffled sounds of several dogs barking but the generator drowned out most other noise. They closed the distance quietly, which was easy to accomplish in the sandy soil. Jack suddenly crouched behind some ferns and Luke quickly did the same. Jack stayed very still for several minutes. Luke could not see a thing except the back of Jack's head and neck. Two mosquitoes were trying to land on Jack's neck, but couldn't because of the repellent. Luke wondered how he could think about those mosquitoes at a time like this.

Jack slowly turned around and whispered, "They have trained dogs guarding their camp. The wind is in our favor or they would have smelled us by now. We'd better not get any closer or we'll risk getting found out."

Jack unbuttoned his shirt and took out a pair of binoculars. Luke could see they were night vision binoculars. Jack stayed on his knees as he raised the binoculars to his eyes and began to scan the camp, starting at the east end and slowly working his way to the opposite side of the camp. Luke remained quiet, waiting for Jack to explain what he saw. Jack kept looking through the binoculars but began telling Luke what he was seeing.

"There are three men down there that I can see," he began. "They've got Buster out of the truck and have chained him close to other dogs. There are three dogs being used as watch dogs to make sure no one surprises this group. They look like two rottweilers and a German shepherd to me. Do you want to have a look?" Jack handed the binoculars to Luke.

Luke had never looked through binoculars like this. He tried to focus on the camp itself, to see if Sam was there. He couldn't see Sam but could see the back side of Buster. Other dogs were barking at him but he remained motionless, probably still sedated, or a bit bewildered at least. He could make out the outlines of three men, the two from the pickup and a third man. They were obviously discussing something about the dogs, because they would occasionally point in the direction of the dogs. Just then a fourth man came out of a cabin and started walking to meet the others. The way he walked signified he was probably the leader. Luke told Jack what he had seen and handed the binoculars back so he could look for himself.

Jack could see the four men talking but couldn't make out a word of their conversation. "That fourth guy does look like the boss," Jack agreed as he continued to look through the glasses. "It looks like they're planning to turn off the generator and go to sleep." The leader started back to his cabin and the other three went to a smaller cabin. One of the three went behind the cabin and stopped the generator. Suddenly all was dark and the only sounds were intermittent barks and growls.

"We'd better get out of here," Jack said as he got to his feet but remained bent over. "Be quiet, Luke. Those dogs can hear us now that the generator's off," he warned as he walked back the way they came. As they went down the hill, Jack quickened his pace. Once behind the crest of the hill, he wasn't worried about being seen, but he didn't speak until they were halfway back to the jeep. Then Jack urged Luke to come alongside as he talked.

"We need to know the lay of the land around their camp. That's what we'll do tomorrow, after we get the tire fixed. We can also get a better look at the camp during the day. Maybe we can get enough information to go to the local authorities after that, but if we don't, we'll figure out how to get what we need." Jack said in his optimistic manner. Luke was becoming more and more confident too, not in his own abilities but those of his uncle. How could a guy Jack's size be so strong? How did he know he'd need night vision binoculars? Luke had a lot of questions but remembered that his dad told him not to ask many questions, especially about Jack's work.

Soon they were back at the jeep. The ride back to the rustic campground was uneventful. They parked the jeep and went into the camper. "I'm going to take a shower and go to bed," Jack said. "Once you've showered, we'll fix your bed. I'll sleep up top," Jack said, pointing to the front of the camper, which overlapped the cab of the truck. "Sit here at the table and we'll get something to drink. I'll turn on the hot water heater." As he flipped a switch Luke could hear the pilot light and the heater begin working. Jack opened the refrigerator and brought out a jug of water. Each took a long drink. "Do you want a Coke?" Jack asked as he opened one for himself. Luke nodded and Jack handed him an aluminum can that seemed exceptionally cold, probably because he had got quite warm on this late-night adventure.

"It seems weird not having to worry about chores," Luke said as he took a swallow of pop.

"That's one habit you'll be glad to get rid of," Jack said, smiling.

Luke thought for a moment before answering. "I just wonder how life would be if I didn't have to work all the time," he said, choosing his words. He didn't want to appear ungrateful, but at the same time he envied other kids in school who didn't have responsibilities.

"I know that growing up on a farm is not an easy life, but it does prepare you for later life," Jack said. "Your dad did extra work so I could do sports, and I'll never be able to repay him for that."

"What sports did you do?" Luke asked.

"I had to pick and choose but finally decided on wrestling and track. I liked all sports but I couldn't let your dad carry the work load at home for the whole school year. Since you're the oldest child, it would be harder for you to be gone during chore time, right?" Jack asked.

"The track coach wants me to go out for track," Luke said, "but I never thought I could, so I never asked Mom and Dad."

Jack thought briefly before answering, trying to say the right thing. "If you were good at track, you might get a scholarship that would help pay for college," Jack said. "Do you want to go to college?"

"I think so," Luke answered, "but I'm not sure what I want to study."

"I'm sure your folks want you to go to college, and there's time to figure out what career you wish to pursue after you get in school," Jack said. "I'll help you figure stuff out. Let's concentrate on what we have to do now to get your dogs back. We'll get up early in the morning and get the tire fixed. Then we'll take a walk around the camp, being careful to keep our distance so the dogs don't hear, see, or smell us. Once we know the terrain around their camp, we can go to the local authorities, provided we have enough information to get them to act. We'd better get cleaned up and get to bed." Jack got up from the table and moved toward the bathroom. He removed his long sleeved shirt, and then his T-shirt, revealing a very muscular upper body, but Luke thought he looked more like a gymnast than a body builder.

Without thinking, Luke asked, "How did you lift that jeep all by yourself?" He was embarrassed as soon as he asked, because he realized it sounded as though he didn't think Jack looked strong enough to accomplish that feat.

Jack laughed, seeing that Luke felt bad about asking. "I guess I'm just naturally strong. The good Lord blessed me in that way and all I've had to do is work at staying in shape so when I call upon my body to do something, it responds.

"When I was a kid they had an arm wrestling tournament. I was just a kid and didn't enter but the guy that won was skinny, with probably thirteen—to fourteen-inch biceps. He beat a guy that looked like a body builder and had eighteen—to nineteen-inch arms. I wondered how it was possible and I still don't have all the answers, but I think muscle density, leverage, and bone and tendon strength have something to do with it. When I wrestled in high school it was amusing to watch my opponents as they sized me up and then look at their faces when we actually started wrestling. They were always surprised and sometimes shocked."

Jack turned to go into the bathroom, and Luke saw two distinct scars on his back. The one over his left shoulder was perhaps two inches long, but the one on his lower right back was at least a six-inch scar that extended from the middle of the back diagonally down toward the right hip. Luke didn't dare ask any questions but was dying to know what happened.

Soon Jack was done showering and came out of the bathroom wearing gym shorts. "That feels better," he said as he climbed into bed. "Go ahead and get your shower. I'll make up your bed while you're doing that."

As Luke showered his thoughts drifted over a range of topics. So much had happened in the past few days. It made him tired, and the shower even relaxed him more. When he came out of the shower the table had been converted to a bed and he barely remembered lying down before he was asleep.

Chapter 11

The camp where Buster had been taken smelled of dog excrement. There were perhaps twenty dogs in camp. Most were chained, but some were in an enclosure between two log cabins, one slightly larger than the other. Slim was glad to finally park the truck after the long day's ride. His partner, Seth, was really too big to be comfortable driving the truck, and Slim didn't trust anyone's driving anyway, especially with his truck. As soon as the truck pulled into camp, three watch dogs came up to make sure Slim and Seth were the ones in the truck. Satisfied, they went back on patrol, stopping briefly to smell the new dog in the back of the truck.

An athletic looking man opened the door of the smaller cabin and came out to meet the two men standing in front of the truck. "It took you long enough," was all he said as he circled the truck, pointing the flashlight into the dog box to see what they had brought.

"We missed you too, Wade" Slim said, irritated that the man didn't have a better greeting for him.

"While you two are driving around, enjoying the countryside, me and Dorsey are busy trying to make something of these sorry dogs you bring us. As long as you were gone, I expected you'd have more than one dog to show for your efforts," Wade said, disgusted with the two men.

"You aren't being very nice, Wade," the big man said. "Me and Slim tried to get more dogs but things just didn't work out. This one's a dandy though, isn't he?"

Wade went around the truck and looked through the two holes of the box with his flashlight again. "He looks like he might have potential, I'll give you that. If he doesn't, he'll be sport for the real fighters," Wade said, chuckling at the thought of Buster being ripped to pieces.

Wade walked back to the cabin to get a leash. When he came back Slim warned him that the dog might bite him, but Wade opened the box and quickly had the leash attached to Buster's collar before Buster could even respond in his groggy state.

"You just don't know how to work with dogs, you little squirt," Wade told Slim as he helped Buster off the truck and tied him to a stake close to the other dogs. The dogs started barking as Buster approached. All the barking made Buster confused, but he didn't react to the other dogs. He just lay down once he was tied to a stake, just out of reach of the nearest dogs, who were also tied to stakes.

"This dog's big enough, but he sure doesn't have any fight," Wade commented as he left Buster and went back where the other two men were standing.

The noise of the barking dogs caused the bigger cabin door to open, revealing a broad man who filled the entire doorway. He was dressed in woodland camo with black, high-top military boots that were very shiny. He wore a floppy camo hat with a strap that hung freely, dangling under his chin. All three men tensed as the fourth man stepped down from the small cabin porch and approached.

"We got a good dog for you, Jim," Slim said, nervously pointing at Buster.

Jim Dorsey looked at Buster, resting quietly while the other dogs kept barking at him. "Is that it?" Dorsey asked, turning back to Slim and Seth.

"We had problems at the other two places we had checked out. This dog came from the same place we got that good fighter from last week," Slim said, hoping to convince Dorsey they had done a good job. "Those farmers sure are dumb, getting a new dog for us to take so soon," Seth added.

"Did you remember to pick up your darts this time?" was all Dorsey had to say in response.

"Yeah, I got it right here in my pocket," the big man replied, reaching into the breast pocket of his shirt and producing the small orange dart, which he held out for his boss to see.

Unimpressed, Dorsey stared at the three men. "I can't make any money if you guys waste all this time driving around the country, and come back with just one dog.

"But it's a good one, Big Jim," Slim said, pointing at Buster to emphasize his point. You can see he has all the qualities of a good fighter."

"I hope you're right," Dorsey said, "or I'm not going to pay you for your time or your gas." "If he turns out to be meat for my fighters, it's going to be your loss. I'm tired of taking all the losses around here."

Slim and Seth knew better than to argue with Jim Dorsey. Even though Seth was bigger, Jim was stronger, smarter, and definitely meaner. Sometimes he bragged about what he'd done to people who crossed him, and there were rumors that he'd killed several people and was proud of it. Slim knew Dorsey well enough to not argue with him, and not even get on his bad side. He'd heard that Dorsey was involved with kidnapping and child pornography, but didn't know for sure and wasn't about to ask. Slim felt that, although he was a thief, he did have some honor and certainly had a conscience, which he was sure Dorsey did not have. He'd seen Dorsey kill a dog for just looking at him in the wrong way, laughing every minute as the life blood drained out of the poor canine. No one liked the way Dorsey treated the dogs or his help, but the pay was decent and it beat factory work, so it was easy to find men to work for him. Once they hired on, it was hard to leave, because the men were afraid to leave. Slim remembered one man who talked about leaving, and suddenly he came up missing. Nothing was said, but Slim thought Dorsey had probably killed him with the big Bowie knife he always had with him—and knew how to use.

Jim Dorsey might have had one weakness. He simply loved (if a man like him could love) his massive brindle-colored, mastiff—Staffordshire terrier cross. The dog was 140 pounds of pure muscle and Dorsey thought the dog was as mean as he was. Maybe that's why he loved the dog. It seemed strange to Slim that a man as mean as Dorsey could act so nice to that dog of his, even sharing food with it and talking to it like a dad talked to his child.

Even Wade was afraid of Dorsey, and Wade was a strong man. But he didn't have a lot of ambition, so he tried to stay on Dorsey's good side, hoping to be included in the profits that might come from their dog fighting business. Seth, although huge, was really a gentle giant, and wasn't smart enough to really understand a lot of things.

Slim's thoughts were suddenly interrupted by Dorsey's deep voice. "Remember, you guys, we've got one week before that fight in Chicago, and I've got some money riding on this new dog. You'd better get to bed. We've got a lot of work to do tomorrow. You didn't bring any liquor into camp with you, did you, boys?" Dorsey asked, taking a step toward Slim and Seth.

Slim automatically backed up a step, saying, "No, we know better than that, Big Jim."

"You'd better not," Dorsey said, cursing. "Now turn off that generator and get some sleep, and try to keep these dogs quiet." He walked back into his cabin, not bothering to look back.

"Dorsey is a hard man to please," Slim said as the men walked to their cabin.

"I wish you two would have brought back more than one dog," Wade said. "Then Dorsey wouldn't be upset with you, and now he's upset with me too."

Wade went behind the cabin and turned off the generator, causing darkness and abrupt silence to fall over the camp. All three men undressed and got into their beds. When Slim was convinced the other two were sleeping, he reached under his mattress and found the fifth of whiskey he had hidden there. If Dorsey ever found out he had whiskey in camp there would be no telling what he'd do to Slim, but Slim needed something to calm his frazzled nerves. His stomach was also bothering him, which he tried to ignore as he silently drank his whiskey. It was one of the few pleasures he had in life, he thought as he replaced the cap on the bottle and gently replaced the bottle under his mattress. Now he should be able to sleep.

Chapter 12

Luke, wake up, Jack said as he tried to gently arouse Luke, who nonetheless awoke with a start. He wasn't used to sleeping so hard.

"What time is it?" Luke asked as he sat up and rubbed his eyes, trying to clear his mind as well as his vision.

"Almost six A.M.," Jack said as he turned to the kitchen sink and started working on breakfast. As Jack prepared breakfast, Luke converted the bed back to a table and soon they were eating eggs and toast. After breakfast they did the dishes and quickly made sure camp was in order before piling into the jeep.

"Munising's only twenty to thirty minutes west of here," Jack explained as they headed back to the highway. "I looked at the county map and have a pretty good idea about the roads around their camp. Not very far to the north is Pictured Rocks, so we know they won't be able to get away by heading north. It looks like there's a creek or small river just west of their camp, and we might use that to get closer to them, if we need to. Once we're able to see what's in the camp, we can tell the sheriff here in Munising and he can take it from there. I could use back roads to get to

Munising but I think I'll just go back to M-28 so we don't get lost and lose valuable time."

Luke looked at the scenery. The terrain looked mostly marshy and swampy at first but changed to rolling hills and hardwoods as they approached Munising. As they entered the town Luke got his first look at Lake Superior, which appeared very calm and gorgeous as the eastern sun reflected off the still water of the bay. A short way out into the bay Luke noticed a large island, which blocked his view of the big lake to the north. This was a very beautiful little town, quaint and friendly looking, Luke thought.

Jack turned left into a service station and told the attendant what he needed. Since it was early in the morning and a week day, they were obviously not busy. The attendant, dressed in blue, oil-stained coveralls, carried the tire into the service area. Jack came back to the jeep to talk to Luke. Luke knew that Jack didn't have to include him in his planning, and he appreciated Jack for doing this, making him feel like a part of the process.

"This is a pretty place, isn't it?" Jack asked as he looked at the lake. Luke nodded but didn't answer. "Pictured Rocks is east of here. They have tour boats that take people out to see the Rocks. We'll have to do that some time." Luke was continually surprised that Jack could take the time to enjoy the beauty of nature, and seem to be so relaxed, when there was so much to do to get the dogs back and get these people locked up.

Luke turned toward the station to see the attendant bringing out the tire. "That was quick. Thanks, and keep the change," Jack said as he paid the attendant and started loading the tire on the back of the jeep. The attendant thanked Jack profusely as he backed toward the entrance of the station. Jack got back into the jeep and quickly pulled unto the highway, heading east. They stopped briefly at an auto parts store to buy a new jack and were on their way again.

Chapter 12

"Let's stop at this grocery and get a few bottles of water. I have a water filter in the camper but I hate to take the time to use it, and we shouldn't be out that long anyway," he said as he pulled into a 7-Eleven. "Do you want a candy bar or anything?" Jack asked as he got out.

"Maybe a Baby Ruth," Luke said.

Jack was gone but a minute before returning with the water and candy bar, which he handed to Luke. "Remind me to take some jerky with us when we get back to the camper," he said as he got in the jeep and once again headed east along M-28 back to camp.

"We'll need to take regular binoculars, two-way radios, water, jerky, a compass, and I'm going to have you take your bow, just in case," Jack said as they pulled into the campground. "It looks like a warm, sunny day so dress appropriately, but take a heavier shirt in case it cools off."

Jack quickly showed Luke how to operate the two-way radio, if they had to separate for any reason. "Don't wear bright colors," Jack warned Luke. "We don't want them to see us walking around their camp." Jack put the things they needed on the table. "Here's the mosquito repellent. If the wind continues from the north, we probably won't need it, and we're going to have to pay attention to the wind. If the wind shifts and those three guard dogs smell us, they'll alert those men, and then come after us." Jack took Luke's bow out of the closet and attached a quiver to it that held three arrows. He removed the arrows from the quiver, unscrewed the target points, and opened a small plastic box and took out three sharp broadheads. He felt each edge with his fingers and ran a file over each edge until he was satisfied they were sharp enough before screwing the broadheads unto the tips of the arrows, placing them in the quiver and handing the bow to Luke. Luke took the bow, but wondered why he would need it since they were just trying to find out more about the thieves' camp.

"You probably won't need the bow, but it's easy to carry and can protect you if circumstances change," Jack said.

After Jack was satisfied with the gear, he reached into a drawer and brought out a small plastic case, which he unlocked. Inside was a shiny hand gun, which Jack picked up and studied briefly before snapping a clip of bullets into the bottom of the grip. He then put the gun in a small holster and arranged it so it was behind him, concealed under his long-sleeved shirt. Luke was beginning to get excited now because he realized for the first time that Jack felt these people were potentially dangerous. Jack, reading his thoughts, told Luke that he didn't intend to use the gun but wanted to have it if something went wrong.

After stepping out of the camper Jack quickly inspected Luke to make sure he had everything he needed. Not satisfied, Jack opened a compartment on the side of the camper and took out a small backpack. He had Luke put the water, jerky, his radio, and binoculars into the backpack.

"Try it on," Jack said as he held it up for Luke, who turned around and placed his arms behind him so Jack could place the straps properly and secure the backpack. "Does it feel comfortable?" Jack asked as he finished adjusting the straps for Luke.

"Yeah," Luke said as he moved his arms and shoulders, adjusting to the light load of the pack. Satisfied, Jack handed Luke his bow, locked the camper, showed Luke where he hid the key, and headed for the jeep. He opened the back end of the jeep so Luke could put his bow and the pack in the back while they traveled the short distance to the trail where the dog thieves were camped. The two then got into the jeep and headed to the two-track, being careful to park far enough away to not arouse suspicion.

Jack parked the jeep off the road 150 yards from the two-track so that it couldn't be seen unless a car drove right by it on the road. He locked the jeep but showed Luke where he put the key—

on top of the front tire on the passenger side—in case he needed to get in.

"Luke, before we get started, I'd like to have a quick word of prayer," Jack said as he faced Luke and put his strong hands on his shoulders. Luke was mildly surprised, but was accustomed to praying with his family at meals and at church. He watched as Jack closed his eyes and began to pray. "My Lord and my God," Jack said. "Thank you for your love for us. I pray for safety for Luke and myself, and that we would make wise decisions. Help us to get Sam and Buster safely away from this place, and I pray that these men would be brought to justice. I pray this in Jesus' name, Amen."

Jack then opened his eyes and looked at Luke, a very serious expression coming over his face. "Your mom and dad entrusted your safety to me, Luke, so I don't want you to do anything to put yourself in jeopardy. If something happens and the situation gets out of control, I want you to come back to the jeep and drive to the camper and wait for me. My cell phone doesn't work well up here, so I can't use it to call the sheriff, so we'll have to go into town and get them."

As he turned to lead the way, he suddenly turned back and said, "Remember to keep track of the wind. Let me see if I can help you." Jack got the key and opened the passenger side and looked in the console briefly, before closing the door and replacing the key on the tire, being careful that it was not visible without bending over to look for it. He then came back and showed Luke a small metal tin of dental floss. He tore off a twelve-inch length. Then he asked Luke to hold his bow while he fastened the floss to the string near the end of the upper limb. Jack proceeded to fray the end of the dental floss so it had many tiny strands at the end, then he watched as the floss was lifted by the slight northerly breeze coming off the lake.

"That's perfect," he told Luke. "If the wind changes and blows from us into their camp, we're in trouble, so get back to the jeep as fast as you can. If I'm not here, start the jeep and head back to the camper. I'll meet you there." Luke could feel his heart quicken as he sensed the excitement and thrill of their endeavor to get their dogs back. He hoped Sam and Buster were safe. Buster was probably safe, because both he and Jack had looked at the monitor earlier and seen the familiar signal.

Luke's mouth was dry, yet he didn't want to take time to drink as the two walked down the road to the two-track.

"Let's explore the west end first," Jack said. Careful not to leave their tracks in the sand, they again stayed off the two-track as they headed northwest, keeping their distance from the camp. They crossed a series of hills and valleys with a mixture of maples and evergreens. The sandy soil made for quiet walking except for the occasional branch that was broken while stepping over it. Luke was glad to be doing something physical and positive to free Sam and Buster. Walking helped him relax and unwind a little, too.

Jack pointed west and showed Luke where he thought a river wound its way northward, eventually emptying into Lake Superior. "If we're on this side of the camp and we need to distance ourselves from their camp, we'll head to the river," he said as they continued northward. The landscape eventually flattened into a mature hardwood forest with pines intermixed. "We're getting close to Pictured Rocks," Jack said. "Their camp is probably one and one-half miles from here and we know they're not coming this way to escape."

"How do you know that?" Luke asked being unfamiliar with the terrain."

"I'll show you," Jack said as he guided Luke closer to the lake. Luke could see the blue sky up ahead as the tree line obviously ended abruptly. As Luke got closer he could see the big lake in the northern horizon. As they got closer still, Luke could see they were actually much higher than the lake. He could hear muffled sounds of waves hitting rocks.

"Watch your step, now," Jack cautioned as they neared the edge. As Luke walked slowly the last few feet to the edge he got his first view of the rugged cliffs with the beautiful weathered rocks. Luke stopped a safe distance from the edge and just stared at the beauty before him. The bright sunlight reflecting brilliantly off the lake contrasted sharply with the shadows down below. Finally, he asked Jack, "How high are we above the lake?"

"A couple hundred feet, I guess. It's beautiful, isn't it? I've seen a lot of this world and I still find this to be one of the most beautiful places on earth," Jack said as he gazed at the rocky cliffs below. "Maybe we can take a tour boat out there and see the whole shoreline. These rocks extend for miles in each direction. Those people in that camp won't be coming this way if they want to get away. They really haven't picked a good spot to camp as they only have one way out, which is the way they came in. Let's get back to their camp," Jack said as he turned to leave. "What direction is the wind?" He asked Luke, testing him.

"Straight out of the north," Luke answered without hesitation, looking at the tip of the bow with the dental floss waving in the breeze.

"Good," Jack said. "Remember to check the wind regularly. I want to find a good vantage point for you to see the camp from the west. I'll probably have you stay there while I go back around and look at the east side of their camp."

They lessened their pace as they reached the perimeter of the camp. Luke could see Jack glimpse at the floss on the tip of the bow.

"Let's stop here and prepare," Jack said as he took off his own small backpack, laid it on the ground, and unzipped the bag. He took out two hand radios and handed one to Luke. "These two radios are on the same frequency and I've got the volume adjusted, so all you have to do to talk is press this button as you speak and let up as I answer. Keep it in your shirt pocket." Jack went through the motions of showing Luke how to operate the radio. It seemed simple enough to Luke but Jack backed off several feet and had Luke test the radio.

Convinced that Luke could operate the radio properly, Jack reached into his backpack and took out a small plastic box that had three colors of face camouflage. Jack quickly put his first three fingers into the corresponding black, gray and brown camo paint and expertly streaked it over his forehead, around his eyes, down his cheek, ending on his neck on the left side. He changed hands and did the same to the right side of his face. Then he turned to Luke and painted his face. "I don't want those guys seeing your smiling white face sticking out of those green ferns," Jack said, explaining his concerns for concealment and safety.

"Now let's get these binoculars out so you can see what's going on in camp while I quickly scout the east side." Jack rummaged through his pack briefly before bringing out a pair of pocket binoculars. "Don't keep these around your neck as it could interfere with shooting the bow if you need to. Keep them in your shirt pocket or your pack when not using them. Leave your stuff here and let's get closer to their camp," he said as he cautiously moved in the direction of the dull sound of the generator.

Jack motioned for Luke to bend down as they got closer, until they both crawled the last few yards to their vantage point, concealed by smaller pines and ferns. Jack slowly parted the ferns to see the camp below him from the slightly elevated hill-top hiding place.

Jack took the binoculars from Luke to survey the camp. He quickly looked to see if he could account for the men. He readily spotted the three men who were doing various camp chores. He recognized "Mutt and Jeff," the two he and Luke had followed up here. The one man was so big he dwarfed the smaller man, making them look like a comical pair. The third man appeared to be of average build, somewhat athletic, with stringy-looking brown hair. None of the men carried weapons and they appeared to be totally unconcerned about anyone finding them. They obviously relied mostly on the three guard dogs to keep watch over the camp and Jack could see all three dogs diligently patrolling the periphery of the camp, stopping occasionally to sniff the air before walking on and looking for something out of the ordinary. Jack could barely hear the sound of dogs occasionally barking.

Switching his attention to the captive dogs, he could feel a silent rage rise inside him. There were perhaps twenty dogs, all tied on very short ropes and chains, just out of biting distance of each other. They did not appear underfed, but that was the only good thing that could be said. Some dogs were lying as far away from other dogs as possible, which was only about six feet in any direction. Other dogs were at full alert, intently staring at those close by, or barking a challenge to any dog that might accept.

Jack had read a little about fighting dog operations but didn't know a lot of the details about what was going on here. Occasionally Jack could smell the odor of canine feces, so he knew the dogs were living in filthy conditions. Obviously the dog thieves could quickly tell who were the most aggressive and dominant dogs by tying all the dogs in close proximity to each other and noting their response. It was obvious there was no real concern for the health of these dogs. Many would be used as a mere "training exercise" for the good fighting dogs, to keep them in fighting condition so the superior fighters would be in the best shape possible to win money for the owner.

Jack hated the thought of using animals like this, and wondered what type of person would do this to these dogs, many taken from loving families, never to be seen again, only to be killed in a horrible manner, just so a few could profit. As he was thinking about this a well-proportioned military type came out of the small cabin. His head was shiny and bald, and he quickly put on a black baseball cap. He wore shiny black military boots with camo pants tucked neatly inside. His long-sleeved woodland camo shirt was tucked into his pants and the sleeves were rolled up past the elbows, revealing powerful forearms. He walked with the confidence of someone in charge.

"Looks like a skinhead," Jack muttered softly as he sized up this potential foe. The man had a hunting knife encased in a leather carrier, which hung from his black belt on his left side. He had a hand gun holstered on his right side. Occasionally the sun would reflect off the metal of the stainless steel gun butt as the leader walked toward the other men.

Jack began to be more concerned about Luke after seeing the handgun but felt that as long as they stayed out of reach all would go well. Luke was trying his best to see if Sam was among the dogs in camp. Jack handed him the binoculars to look for Sam as he continued to follow the leader as he walked from one man to the next, obviously giving orders he expected to be followed.

After he talked to his men he went back to the cabin briefly, only to come out with a huge, thickly muscled fighting dog. He had him on a tight leash that was buckled to a thick leather collar with metal spikes sprouting from it. As the man walked the dog close to the other tied dogs, some barked, but most quit barking, sat down, and were submissive to this huge canine as he got closer. Not one dog challenged him. It was obvious from a distance that the skinhead was proud of his dog. He then turned to the three men, who had stopped their chores to watch their leader, and shouted in a deep raspy voice, much like that of a professional wrestler, "Tomorrow we'll see if the new arrival will give Champ any competition."

Luke turned to Jack, clearly concerned about Buster's safety.

Sensing Luke's concern, Jack said, "Don't worry, we'll have them in custody by then." Jack then focused on the wind direction, which was still out of the north. He watched the guard dogs for several minutes as they patrolled. Two were heavily muscled Rottweilers and the other was a sleek German shepherd, not quite as heavily muscled but obviously well conditioned.

Satisfied with what he saw, Jack turned to Luke. "Keep an eye on the wind at all times. Radio me if you need to talk. If something goes wrong, head for the river or the jeep." My cell phone won't work in this area, so we can't call the sheriff like we planned. I'll go check out the east side of camp and then we'll go into town and get the county sheriff to help us out. I think we have enough evidence to get them to help us, but I want to make sure they can't escape to the east or northeast if they try to leave. Do you have any questions?"

Luke could feel his heart rate go up as he looked into Jack's face. Jack looked serious, but you could see the hint of a smile as he looked at Luke. "No, I'll stay here while you're scouting and radio if there's a problem."

"Good," Jack said. "I'll call regularly and shouldn't be gone more than thirty minutes." Jack patted Luke on the shoulder and backed away from their vantage point in a crouched position before standing and walking back to the south. Soon his form was swallowed by the trees and Luke was alone. He put the binoculars to his eyes and continued his search for Sam and Buster. As he gazed upon the dogs tied to their stakes he felt sorry for them. They were filthy, and most probably came from homes that were missing them as much as he missed Sam. He even felt a little guilty for getting Buster into this predicament, as he would surely be killed by the skinhead's huge dog, if not by one of the other dogs. Sam was not in that group of dogs, but there was a small enclosed area between the cabins that he couldn't see into. The steady drone of the generator made it impossible to hear accurately, but once in awhile he thought he heard dogs barking in that enclosure. Several minutes passed as Luke kept searching for his dogs. Jack's voice came over the radio. Luke was so intent in his searching that the sudden noise scared him and he jumped as Jack began speaking, even though the volume was very low.

"Luke, I'm over on the east side of their camp and heading north. The terrain is much the same as the west side but no river. I'll continue north for awhile and check that out. Do you copy?"

Luke started to say something but stopped himself, realizing he had to depress the button as he spoke. He took the radio from his pocket and held it in his left hand, depressing the black button with his thumb. "Yes, I hear you," Luke began, feeling a bit odd as he never used a two-way radio before. "I don't see any sign of Sam or Buster," he continued. "I see an enclosed area by those cabins and it sounds like there may be some dogs in there. Do you hear me?"

There was a short period of silence as Luke looked at the radio, expecting an answer. "Yes, I hear you," came the reply. "I can see that enclosure better from this side and it does sound like dogs are in there. Just stay where you are and keep an eye on things. I'll be back shortly. Over and out." Luke looked at the little radio briefly, trying to decide where to put it as it felt too bulky in his shirt pocket. He finally decided to put in on his belt, as it had a clip on the back, probably designed for that very purpose. He picked up the binoculars and began watching the camp again.

Luke spent the next several minutes looking through the binoculars. Suddenly the radio sounded again.

"Luke, the wind has changed. Get back to the jeep, fast. Do you copy?"

Luke picked up his bow and looked at the little piece of floss as it drifted in the air current toward the camp.

"Yes, I hear you. I'm leaving now," Luke said, surprised at the urgency in Jack's voice.

Chapter 13

In the camp, Big Jim Dorsey was still in a foul mood. He had looked Buster over and was convinced he didn't have the heart of a fighter. "This whole week has been a waste," he proclaimed, looking at Slim and Seth, shaking his head in disapproval. Neither man dared look at Big Jim for fear he would take that as a challenge to his authority. Slim was beginning to hate Jim Dorsey, and he already hated this job, but he didn't know how to get out of this situation. If he just left, Dorsey said he'd track him down and kill him, and he believed he would, too.

Slim's thoughts were cut short by Dorsey's deep voice. "You guys finish your work and then let's give that dog you brought here last week a workout. He needs something to tune him up for the Chicago fights. We'll put him with that sorry black lab cross you got from Battle Creek. It probably won't last long, but it'll help my new fighter remember what he's here for." The thought of a fight made Wade smile as he finished his work. He was bored and needed a little diversion from an otherwise dreary day, he thought as he ran a dirty hand through his dirty blond hair.

Dorsey was headed back to his cabin, leaving the three men to finish their work. The three men went about their tasks for the next several minutes. Slim just happened to look up in time to see Duke, one of the Rottweilers, smell something in the air. He whined a little, and charged off toward the southwest. Slim watched for a minute, waiting for the dog to return, but he didn't. Soon the other rotweiller, patrolling across the camp, sniffed the air and quickly ran off in the direction Duke had gone.

"Seth, Wade, something's wrong," Slim said in his nervous voice.

"What's wrong now, wimp?" Wade asked, coming over to see what was bothering the skinny little guy. As he walked closer to Slim, Wade saw the German shepherd tear off toward the southwest, whining and yipping with excitement.

"Dorsey," Wade yelled, "the dogs are onto something." Dorsey poked his head out of his cabin, trying to see what was going on. "The dogs took off in that direction," Wade said, pointing his arm stiffly toward the southwest.

"Well, go get them and see what they're after. I hope it's not one of those tree hugging hikers from the national park. Those dogs will kill him, if you don't get there fast. All three of you, go, now. I'll stay here and look after things. Hurry! I'll turn off the generator so we can hear better." In a flash, all three men were running through the woods, with Seth bringing up the rear.

As Luke looked around to make sure he had everything, he glanced back at the camp in time to see one of the Rottweilers sniff the air and quickly head right for him. Luke's heart raced as he started running to the south. He knew the dog would catch him before he got to the jeep so he decided to head west. Maybe he could make it to the river before the rotweiller caught him. Luke didn't have time to radio Jack as he turned to the west and ran as fast as he could, breaking old pine branches as he ran through the trees.

Chapter 13

As fast as he ran, Luke soon could hear the big dog behind him. He knew he would never reach the river, so he instinctively changed his course as he spotted a clearing to the north, just twenty-five yards ahead. He got to the clearing in seconds and ran to the far end before stopping and turning. He quickly took an arrow from his quiver, and forced himself to focus on nocking the arrow, even though he could hear the dog, perhaps fifty yards away from the other side of the clearing and coming fast. Luke couldn't see the dog as he raised the bow. He was scared but really didn't have time to give in to that emotion. He wondered what the dog would do when he saw him. Maybe he would stop long enough for Luke to get a shot at him. Luke looked around quickly, thinking he could climb a tree, but there were no trees big enough in the immediate area. He looked back to see the big black and tan dog enter the clearing. The dog stopped briefly as he spotted Luke, growled viciously, and charged with his mouth open, intent on mauling the young man. Luke already had drawn the bow halfway and simply continued to draw, all the while looking at that giant head coming for him. The dog was half way through the clearing and probably only thirty feet from Luke when he released the string, sending the arrow deep into the open mouth of the approaching dog.

This seemed to infuriate the dog as he tumbled over and over, writhing in pain, trying desperately to get the arrow from his mouth, kicking up sand and old pine needles as he struggled. Luke stood in a trance at the scene before him. Bright red blood covered the face, neck and shoulders of the dog, causing sand and pine needles to stick to his hair. As the dog struggled in the clearing Luke drew another arrow, waiting for the dog to charge again. As the rottweiler continued to tumble over and over in the clearing, Luke saw the arrow break off where it entered the dog's mouth. This caused the dog to stop struggling as it pawed at his mouth, blood and sand intermingled and matted all over his head and face except for the brown eyes, which seemed to begin to refocus on Luke.

Luke drew back the bow and shot again before the dog could charge. This arrow hit the center of the right eye, the broadhead driving deeply into the brain. Luke heard the dog whine for an instant before flexing his neck into a contorted position. Then the dog's muscles relaxed and he stretched out on his side as if he were stretching his muscles before getting up after sleeping, except he wouldn't be getting up again. The huge muscles twitched briefly as the legs and neck extended. The body quivered one final time and then lay limp in the clearing, the arrow pointing at Luke from where the eye had been.

Luke couldn't believe what had just happened. For a moment he thought about the life he had just taken. That dog was just doing what he was trained to do, so Luke felt no hatred for this dog that probably would have killed him.

Luke was still trying to take in all that just happened when he heard brush breaking back toward the camp. Another dog was on its way, and Luke only had one arrow left. He turned around and desperately looked for a tree to climb in, but was afraid he wouldn't be able to find one before the next dog was on him. He turned back just as another rottweiler entered the clearing. This one also stopped briefly before focusing on Luke, gathering himself to charge. Luke hadn't even begun to get his last arrow out of the quiver before the dog started for him. He grabbed for the arrow but knew he had no time to nock it and draw the bow. He turned back to the dog, grasping the arrow like a small spear, throwing the bow to the ground.

Luke was in the process of gripping the arrow when he saw movement to his right. It was Jack running into the clearing to intercept the charging dog. The dog saw Jack at the same time Luke did, and swerved to attack Jack without breaking stride. Jack must have anticipated what was happening because he already had his long-sleeved shirt off and wound around his left forearm to protect him. In his right hand he had a knife with a four-inch blade. As the dog closed in, Jack crouched low to the ground, his left arm up, his body angling forward in anticipation of the force of the dog's charge. The dog grabbed at Jack's forearm and just as quickly Jack plunged the knife into the dog's neck, working the blade to cause as much cutting damage as possible. Blood instantly gushed out of the wound, splattering on Jack as the dog continued to work on Jack's arm, oblivious to the mortal wound inflicted on him.

In a matter of just a few seconds Luke could see the dog weaken and then collapse, still clinging to Jack's shirt and forearm. Jack quickly pried the mouth open and pulled his arm away. He turned to Luke. "Go north, closer to the cliffs, and climb into one of those maple trees before the third dog finds us."

Luke stood, transfixed by the sight of Jack. He had blood all over the front of him, the red even more brilliant against his white T-shirt. He did not appear hurt in the least, and actually seemed very calm, which made Luke feel less afraid, but even as he thought about these things, he caught a glimpse of the third dog coming through the trees heading for the clearing. Jack saw him too and quickly unwound his shirt, bunching it around his left hand. As he did this, Luke realized Jack didn't have his knife although his gun was still in its holster behind him.

The large German shepherd stopped briefly at the far side of the clearing to focus on Jack, who was already crouched with his left arm slightly extended, much like a college wrestler stands when ready for a match to begin. The German shepherd was not as heavy as the rottweiler but was long and muscular and looked very menacing as it focused on Jack and attacked.

As the dog came on him, Jack extended his left hand and the dog grabbed the shirt. Jack lifted the dog's head with his left hand and grabbed the exposed throat with his right hand. He instantly took his left hand out from the wadded up shirt, which the dog was biting furiously, and grabbed the dog's throat with that hand and began choking. The dog quickly flung the shirt aside and rose up, trying to bite Jack, a gurgled growl coming from deep inside him. As the dog stood upright Jack did too, and for a moment Luke thought it looked just like two men fighting, because of the upright position of Jack and the dog. The dog's head moved from side to side, his mouth open, saliva flying in all directions. Jack maintained his death grip and Luke could see the dog fighting for air and beginning to panic. As he panicked, he started flailing his body, which almost made Jack lose his balance as he tilted forward. He quickly regained his footing and continued holding the dog at arm's length. As the dog began to weaken, Jack threw the dog to the ground while still holding the throat and lifted his legs in the air slightly, before driving his right knee down on the rib cage of the dog. He repeated this maneuver several times and Luke could see blood begin to come from the nose and mouth of the once ferocious dog.

Satisfied that it was safe to let go, Jack loosened his grip and backed away from the huge dog. The dog struggled to regain his feet but flopped onto his side each time, as he coughed and gurgled blood into the already blood-stained arena that used to be a sandy clearing in the woods. Soon the dog ceased trying to rise and just lay on his side, his chest heaving as he tried to get air. Luke could see the dog's eyes as they turned from menacing to frightened, and then became transfixed as he stopped breathing. Luke could see the pupils dilate and the dog completely relax, blood gently dripping onto the sand from his moist nostrils.

Luke was shocked at the savage violence he had just witnessed. Before him lay three dogs, dead in a matter of a few minutes. The quietness that this place normally provided was now the scene of death. He couldn't help but think about stories of how the gladiators had fought wild animals to the death; only he was alive, and for that he was very thankful. Jack was already picking up his shirt and looking for his knife when he heard the generator turn off. Finding his knife, which was covered with bloody sand, he picked it up and wiped it on his pants before inspecting it and blowing some small particles away from the base of the blade. Then he folded it and put it in his pocket. He went to the side of the clearing and picked up his backpack before coming over to meet Luke, who had gathered all his stuff as he watched Jack.

"Are you all right?" Jack asked in his calm voice.

"I'm fine, Uncle Jack. How about you?" Luke asked, looking at his left forearm. There were some obvious puncture wounds oozing blood, but Jack moved his wrist and fingers and proclaimed himself fine.

Chapter 14

We gotta get out of here, Jack said, remembering that the generator noise had stopped. Those boys will be looking for their dogs, and I'm going to want you in a safe place when they come looking. When they find these dogs, they're either going to pack up and leave quickly or come after us. We also have to remember that the skinhead has a dog too. Let's go north and get closer to the river."

Jack took off at a run, Luke following as best he could. They quickly covered half a mile and were close to the river and the cliffs when Jack stopped to look around. Luke was breathing quite heavily, but he noticed that Jack wasn't even breathing hard. He wondered how this could be. "He doesn't get tired, and he's strong as an ox." Luke wondered if he were human or some sort of robot with human flesh covering his automated parts.

"Let's go into that grove of trees," Jack said, pointing toward a small group of maples surrounded on three sides by old downfalls and brush. "It'll make a good spot for us to see what develops. Maybe we can surprise these guys if they decide to come after us. Above all else, Luke, you keep yourself safe. Don't worry about me. This is what I do for a living." Luke could see Jack was sorry he'd said that as he quickly turned and started trotting toward the trees. Luke wondered what type of work Uncle Jack did that would put him into dangerous situations on a routine basis. He thought about the CIA or FBI, but didn't know enough about those agencies to know if this was the type of work they did. He did know one thing. He was glad Jack was on his side.

The grove of trees provided some security, since the men wouldn't be able to walk through the thick brush and downfalls along the river so they could concentrate on the area to the south east where they had just come from. Best of all, this place was slightly elevated, and offered a good vantage point. Jack and Luke would be able to see the men approach for at least two hundred yards because the dense woods they had come from opened up into a more mature woods as they got closer to the lake. Jack pointed to a large pine tree at the edge of the grove and told Luke he should climb that tree if he needed to get out of harm's way quickly. But if he needed to distance himself from the thieves, Jack said, Luke should get to the other side of the river, follow the river south for a mile or so and then cross the river and get back to the jeep.

Luke understood what Jack was saying, but was afraid the men would simply go back to their camp, get all the dogs, and leave.

"Those men aren't likely to leave until they find out who killed their dogs," Jack explained. "They don't have a truck big enough to transport all those dogs at one time either. They didn't plan very well, did they?" Jack smiled as he looked back the way they had come from.

Luke looked at Jack, who was covered in dried blood. His face had a few splotches on it but his whole front and both arms were dark red. As the blood dried on his arms it began to crack and flake. Jack took off his T-shirt and threw it into the brush. He then proceeded to get a handful of sand and rub it on his bloody skin in an effort to wipe off the dried blood. This was amazingly effective and in a short time Jack was fairly clean.

"I think it was Geronimo who used to take sand baths," Jack said. "You've probably seen dogs and cats roll in the dirt or sand, right?" Luke had seen several animals do that but had not given it much thought.

Jack then put on his long-sleeved shirt, which had several small tears from dog bites. It was amazing that the shirt wasn't completely shredded, Luke thought. Jack buttoned the heavy denim shirt and tucked the bottom inside his pants. "I want you to stay here while I go back and make sure these guys don't get away. They could just abandon the camp and take off, but I doubt they would do that. They have no reason to come in this direction unless they're trailing us, and I'm going to go back and surprise them if that's what they're doing," Jack told Luke. "I'm going to leave my pack here with you, and I'll be back to get you soon. Let's make sure our radios still work," he said as he took his radio out of his pack and spoke into it. Luke tested his radio also and they both put the radios on their belts.

Jack could tell Luke didn't want to stay by himself, but knew he would obey orders. "Your folks are going to be real upset with me as it is," Jack explained. "That dog was going to tear you up. I'm glad you learned to shoot that bow. It probably saved your life. You've only got one arrow left, I see. You likely won't need to use it, but if you do, shoot straight." Luke looked at the bow and arrow. It seemed to be in good shape, he thought as he turned it from side to side to inspect it.

Satisfied that they were again prepared, Jack told Luke to sit behind a large maple tree and watch the area they had come from. Once Luke was situated, Jack looked him in the eye, smiled and winked and started trotting back the way they had just come from. Luke could see Jack trotting for at least two hundred yards but then he disappeared into the pines where the hardwood forest stopped and gave way to the smaller trees. Luke realized Jack would be safe, and he only wished he could see what happened if those men tried to mess with him.

The rays of sun filtering through the big maple trees in bright bands brought a stirring beauty to this place. It was quiet and peaceful, but then Luke remembered the peaceful clearing where three dogs met their death, and it made him wonder if this place would be the scene of more conflict.

Once Jack got to the smaller pine trees he stopped to listen. Hearing nothing, he cautiously moved through the trees toward the clearing where he had fought the dogs. He knew that when the men found the dogs they probably would find tracks where he and Luke had departed. If they followed those tracks, they were in for a surprise, Jack thought to himself. He wasn't worried about three of the four men, but that skinhead could be trouble. He hoped the four men would split up, or at least not be all together when he confronted them. As he moved closer to the clearing, he formulated a plan that would split the men up, or at least space them out a little, so he could confront them one at a time. As he moved slowly and silently closer to the clearing he heard voices, at first quiet, but then raised in bewilderment and anger.

Jack finally could see the clearing up ahead and three men leaning over the dead dogs, inspecting them for any signs of life. The smallest man, who had driven the pickup with Buster, was the most distressed. He talked in a high-pitched voice. "When Dorsey sees this, he's going to be mad, real mad. We gotta find who did this or he might take it out on us," he said as he looked from the dogs to his two comrades. They appeared to ignore him and started to look around the clearing.

"Look, here's some tracks," one said as he pointed to the tracks Jack and Luke had made as they left the clearing.

None of the men appeared to have weapons, probably because they weren't expecting this kind of trouble, and they obviously didn't want to go back to their camp for guns. As the three men focused on the tracks leading out of the clearing, Jack stepped out from his hiding place fifty yards away. The small man spotted Jack instantly.

"There he is!" he shouted as all three looked at Jack, who took off at an awkward trot, partially dragging his right leg.

"He's hurt," Jack could hear one say, which is what he'd hoped they would think. He looked behind him and saw all three men start running after him, cursing as they swore vengeance on him for what he had done to their dogs.

Jack headed west at a pace that would keep them from catching him, but slow enough to stay close, so they could catch a glimpse of him occasionally through the small pine trees. The big man fell behind quickly but chased as best he could, perhaps fearful of what might happen if they let this man get away. After covering about six hundred yards, Jack could see only the small man following. He figured the huge man was far behind and the second man was somewhere in between, but he didn't know how close he might be, so he looked for a clearing. He thought he would stop and fight the small man at the other side of the clearing and still be able to see the second man coming if he entered the clearing.

He kept running for another hundred yards before finding a clearing suitable for his plan. He limped through the clearing and waited, obscured by two small pine trees. Soon the first man came through the clearing, slowing his pace as he looked for tracks in the sand. Seeing them he ran through the clearing and the last thing he remembered seeing was Jack's fist coming right at his face as he ran right into the punch. The force of the blow knocked him backwards, his feet flying in the air. Jack quickly looked him over to make sure he hadn't killed him. The man's nose was broken, both eyes were swelling shut even as he was being examined, and he was bleeding from the mouth. Jack moved him on his side so he wouldn't choke on his own blood. As he did, two teeth fell out of the man's mouth. Jack dragged the thin man between two small pines, where he would be hidden, and waited for the next man to arrive.

He didn't have long to wait. The second man, bigger and more athletic, stopped at the beginning of the clearing. Seeing the tracks, he yelled back to his partner, in a deep voice, "Seth, he went this way. Hurry up." Then he started through the clearing. He almost made it through the clearing before he glanced to his right and saw Slim's boot. Instantly he knew something was wrong and turned his head back toward the direction the tracks had gone.

There was Jack, standing six feet away. The man's surprise quickly turned to anger and he roared a few obscenities before rushing at Jack. Jack ducked at the last moment and moved to one side as the man grabbed at him as he passed by. As soon as he had passed, Jack grabbed his hand with his own and quickly pushed his fingers backwards. He could hear the bones break, and could even feel the flesh give way without the bony support. The man roared in pain and instinctively bent over. Jack then kicked him in the side with enough force to knock the larger man off his feet. The man couldn't yell because the breath was knocked out of him. He tried to right himself and he turned his head slightly, but quickly lost consciousness as Jack hit him squarely in the face.

Jack looked back at the clearing but the big man hadn't arrived yet, so he turned to move his second victim. He had dragged him only a few feet when the third man entered the clearing. Jack quickly stood up and started walking toward the man. The big man was a bit confused. First, Jack wasn't limping anymore. Second, Jack acted like he was taking a walk in the park, not like he was looking for a fight. And third, Jack did not look like anyone the big man couldn't handle. The only thing that made the man sure that Jack was the right man was the dried blood on his pants and shirt.

The man didn't like the way Jack acted, almost disrespectful.

Chapter 14

"Stop right there," the big man told Jack as he was only ten feet away. "What happened to Wade and Slim?"

Jack stopped momentarily. "Are those your friends, Seth?" he asked with a smile. The big man acted surprised. The arrogance of that smile made the big man furious. He ran toward Jack and drew back his right fist and let fly. It would have killed Jack if it had landed, but instead all he hit was air. Jack had ducked, moved to one side, and delivered a heavy kick to the outer part of the big man's right knee. The big man roared in pain as ligaments tore. He drew back his arm again to try to hit Jack but Jack grabbed the arm and straightened it as he forced it backward further and further, until a popping sound told Jack the shoulder was dislocated. It was obvious there was no fight left in this man, as he fell to the ground, writhing in pain.

Jack waited briefly until the man's groaning lessened before speaking to him. "I'll be back to pick you up shortly, Seth. Don't move so much and it won't hurt near as bad. We'll get you to a doctor. Do you know where your boss is?" The big man grimaced and groaned but tried to look at Jack.

"I don't know. He was back at camp when we came after the dogs," he said, his rapid, shallow breathing making it difficult to speak.

After assuring the man he would be taken care of, Jack started running back to the north. He was worried that the skinhead might find Luke, so he ran as fast as he could, figuring he was probably a mile away from Luke, and he'd already been gone twenty to thirty minutes.

Chapter 15

While all this was happening, Luke maintained his vigil from his vantage point behind the maple tree, totally oblivious to everything except his own thoughts and the stiff northerly breeze that was cooling him. He listened intently but heard only the wind and the occasional wave hitting the rocks far below. Then he thought he heard something else. It was so faint he couldn't tell what it was, so he strained his eyes and cupped his hands behind his ears. Yes, he heard it again. It sounded like a bark, coming from the camp. He continued to listen intently and heard another bark, closer this time. Luke grabbed his bow and held it upright. The floss blew toward the camp.

Luke suddenly realized the danger he was in. The dog he heard must be the skinhead's big dog. He quickly got up and ran through the thick brush and downfalls directly behind him. He made his way through the brush as fast as he could and was slightly relieved when he saw the river before him as he topped a small rise. He made a desperate run down the bank to the river and plunged in. The current was swift but the river wasn't very deep and Luke quickly crossed to the other side. He feared for his life and was trying to decide if he should shoot the dog with the only arrow he had left as it swam across the river, or should he get to higher ground and climb a tree. While he thought about what to do he could hear the dog in the brush on the other side of the river.

Desperate, Luke looked for a suitable tree to climb. Looking to the north, he saw a pine, perhaps a hundred and fifty yards away, close to the cliffs. He wasted no further time, running as fast as he could, his body pushing through the thick brush that lined the river. He didn't dare take time to turn around, and just focused on the tree ahead.

"God, help me!" Luke pleaded as he fought through the brush, branches, and blow downs. He could hear the dog clearly now, whining in anticipation, less than one hundred and fifty feet behind him.

Luke spotted a limb perhaps eight feet in the air protruding from the pine. He forged ahead, using his hands as well as his feet to climb the final hill leading to the pine tree. He tossed his bow aside as he knew he wouldn't have time to shoot and it would hinder his ability to climb. He had a hard time thinking clearly because of the fear of the viscous dog behind him. Finally reaching the tree, Luke jumped up and grabbed the limb. As he attempted to swing his leg over the limb, the limb suddenly broke and Luke fell, his back landing hard on the sandy hillside. His chest and back burned as he tried to gasp for breath that would not come. When he fell, his body landed so that his head was downhill from his feet. Luke opened his eyes briefly to the now up-side-down world. The dog was almost upon him.

Luke closed his eyes in unspeakable terror, waiting for the inevitable. He could hear the dog sniffing around his head, but the dog didn't bite him. Maybe he should play dead, he thought, but he was breathing too hard for that.

Slowly he opened his eyes. The only thing he saw was a large black muzzle pressed close to his head. Luke tried to focus beyond the muzzle and noticed the dog wasn't the color of the big brindle of the skinhead. Focusing harder, he saw the large head of another dog. It was Sam!

"Sam," was all Luke could say. The dog responded by licking his face several times. Finally, Luke moved onto his stomach and raised himself to his knees. Sam came closer and Luke hugged him long and hard. The relief of not being killed and of seeing Sam was overwhelming, and Luke cried openly and unashamedly.

Finally regathering his mental facilities, Luke looked Sam over for signs of illness or injury. Several scabs peppered his back and sides but none appeared serious. Sam's tail wagging uncontrollably told Luke he was happy to be reunited with his friend. Convinced that Sam was fine, Luke took the two-way radio off his belt to call Jack, but found that it wasn't working. Probably because it got wet in the river, Luke concluded. Standing up, he readjusted his backpack, retrieved the bow he had tossed aside earlier, and started back toward the maple tree.

"We'd better go back to where Uncle Jack left me, Sam," Luke said, thinking Jack might have a hard time finding him otherwise. "Let's cross the river and go back up the hill." Luke led the way, Sam content to follow.

After they crossed the river with its refreshing coolness, Luke led the way up the steep, sandy bank. He had to walk sideways to maintain his footing, but finally came over the crest of the embankment, only fifty feet from the cliffs and probably a hundred yards from the maple tee. Luke had just turned to walk toward the maple tree when Sam let out a low, sustained growl.

Luke stopped and Sam stepped out in front of him in a protective gesture. Luke looked around and at first didn't see anything, but then the large bulk of the camouflaged skinhead stepped out from behind a large pine, followed by the huge canine, who, once clear of the tree, lunged forward toward Luke and Sam. The skinhead issued a command in German, and the dog whined and sat down at the end of his heavy leather leash, which the man held tightly wrapped around his left hand. Luke looked around him briefly to see what he could do to help himself, but the large man and dog were too close to try to run.

"Who are you, boy?" the skinhead asked in the deepest voice Luke had ever heard. Even his voice was scary, Luke thought, let alone the implication of the tone of voice. Gathering courage, Luke stood straight and defiantly faced the man.

"I'm Luke Larson and this is my dog, Sam, the one you stole almost two weeks ago. I've come to take him back home," Luke said with the courage of the innocent.

The man looked sternly at Luke for perhaps ten seconds before talking. "First of all, he's not your dog," he said in his bass voice, but he wasn't yelling this time. "Second," he continued, "I can assure you you're not going home." As he said this a cruel and hideous smile came over his face.

"You've cost me money, you little twerp," the man explained. "That dog with you is a good fighting dog, and would have made a lot of money for me, but now I'm going to let my dog have his way with him." As he finished talking he reached down and unsnapped the heavy leash. He issued a single word, again in German, and the dog sprang forward. At the same time, Sam ran forward to meet the huge, brindle-colored beast.

The collision was spectacular! There was vicious growling and snarling as the two dogs locked in a life-and-death struggle, each trying to secure a lethal grip on the other's throat. The two dogs moved so quickly round and round that it was difficult to even see one dog apart from the other, even though Sam had a darker color coat. Luke at first stood mute, but then started yelling for the man to stop the fight. The skinhead stood relaxed against the pine tree, the same sadistic smile etched on his face.

The two dogs continued to struggle, neither falling to the ground. Luke was surprised that Sam could do even this well against the much bigger attack dog, although he was sure Sam would be killed eventually.

Suddenly, the bigger dog made a different type of sound, and Luke could see Sam clinging to the ventral part of the larger dog's neck. Once Sam had cocked his head and neck at such an unusual angle to secure his bite, the bigger dog was able to lift Sam off his feet and shake him like a rat or a stuffed toy, but Sam held on. Sam's face was covered with blood and the actions of the bigger dog became more frantic and it was obvious he was losing strength.

Luke happened to glance at the skinhead. His smile had faded, and he was reaching behind him, bringing a pistol up to the ready position. Although Luke yelled at the man not to shoot, the skinhead continued to try to aim for Sam. The movement of the dogs was still so fast and furious he couldn't get a clear shot. When it became obvious that his dog was not going to survive if he didn't shoot, he picked a spot as best as he could and fired.

The shot had no immediate effect but, seconds later the huge dog collapsed with Sam still growling and shaking his head, not wanting to let go of his neck hold on the bigger dog. Seeing that he had killed his own dog, the skinhead took deliberate aim at Sam, and would have fired, but suddenly a blur came from the south, hitting the man and knocking the gun from his hand. It was Jack, who quickly got up and kicked the gun over the bank leading down to the river.

Surprised, the skinhead focused on the newcomer fifteen feet away. Sizing him up, he reached behind him again and brought out the large bowie knife, which he held in front of him for Jack and Luke to see.

"First, I'm going to kill you," he said, pointing at Jack, "and then I won't even tell you what I'm going to do to the boy." This statement, and what it implied, made Jack very mad, and it was obvious by the way he answered.

"First," Jack said, mimicking the skinhead, "you're not going to hurt anybody, and second, you're going to jail for all the pain you've caused both people and animals." As he said this he got into his crouch position with his arms and hands pointing toward the bigger man, anticipating the upcoming battle. Luke noticed that Jack's pistol was not in the back holster, as it had been earlier.

The skinhead must not have been impressed with Jack because he came forward, trying to get closer. His sadistic smile had returned with the thought of killing Jack, and Jack looked deeply into his blue eyes, seeing the hate and anticipation of inflicting pain and suffering mingle as one into an expression Jack had seen many times before.

The skinhead slashed the knife back and forth several times as he got close to Jack. It was obvious he was well trained and very agile for his size, but Jack was able to avoid the knife by maintaining a low wrestler's stance and moving his feet defensively as the man came forward. Again the man swung the knife, this time coming dangerously close to Jack, but as the knife passed harmlessly by, Jack grabbed the man's right wrist with his left hand while he hit the man hard with his right hand, landing a solid blow to the side of the head.

The skinhead reacted violently and took on a surprised look as he could not get loose from Jack's iron grip. Jack then quickly kicked him in the groin, and the man doubled over in pain, but seemed to recuperate quickly and began fighting with renewed vigor. Jack grabbed the man's other arm before he could strike and the two men fell to the ground, rolling over several times.

As they fought, Luke stood silent, transfixed by the sight before him. He knew this was a life-and-death fight, and he didn't know how to help Jack. He didn't want to go to look for the gun and leave Jack, and he was too engrossed in the fight to think of other alternatives. He was getting worried because Jack and the skinhead were just a few feet from the cliff. If they fell, they would land on the rocks two hundred feet below.

Jack must have sensed the danger and quickly let loose of the skinhead's left hand with a quick maneuver that ended with Jack's left leg over the skinhead's right arm Jack used both hands to push the skinhead's right arm up, hyper extending it until the man shrieked in pain and let go of the knife. Jack used his feet to push himself away from the man. He quickly picked up the knife and tossed it over the cliff as he regained his feet. The skinhead was able to get about halfway to a standing position before Jack began hitting him with both fists, first with the left hand, then the right. The sound of Jack's hand hitting the man's head made Luke feel a little squeamish. The man never regained his feet and finally fell to the ground.

Jack stood over him for a moment before backing away a few feet. He was still dangerously close to the cliff, but turned to see how Luke was doing.

"I'm fine, Uncle Jack," Luke said enthusiastically. "Sam found me." He pointed to Sam, who was less than twenty feet away, sitting calmly on his haunches, apparently observing the fight. Jack began looking for his gun but hadn't even taken one step before he heard Sam growl at the same instant Luke screamed, "Behind you!"

Jack turned in time to see the big man regain his feet. He had pulled a small revolver out of an ankle holster while he was lying down and now he pointed it at Jack. The man still had that hatred in his eyes, but his face and head and eyes were all bloodied and swollen, and dark sand covered much of his once shiny bald head.

The skinhead would have pulled the trigger, even as Jack moved toward him to grab the gun, but Sam came between Jack and the skinhead, flying through the air and hitting the skinhead in the chest, knocking him backward. Jack reached out to grab Sam by the collar but only could grab his right rear leg above the hock, as he passed by. Nevertheless, he had a firm hold of Sam. The skinhead was now leaning over the cliff, facing Jack and frantically grabbing for Sam's collar. Sam would have none of that, and bit the skinhead as his hand came close to his face. Terror briefly came over the skinhead's face before he disappeared over the cliff.

The force of Sam's charge had carried him over the cliff edge too and Jack tried to get some sort of hold on solid ground so he could save Sam. In desperation he grabbed an old pine root and hung on as he too began to slip over the edge of the cliff. Luke could not see Sam from his vantage point but rushed to help Jack. Then he could see Jack holding Sam by one leg.

Jack saw Luke coming and said calmly, "Lie down and wrap your legs around that pine tree behind you." Luke quickly obeyed. "Now grab my wrist with both hands and hang on while I try to swing Sam up to you." When Jack was satisfied that Luke would be safe, he exerted himself one last time and swung Sam up over the edge of the cliff with his right arm. Sam's body landed right next to Luke. Jack was then able to climb up on top of the cliff and soon all three were a safe distance from the edge.

Chapter 16

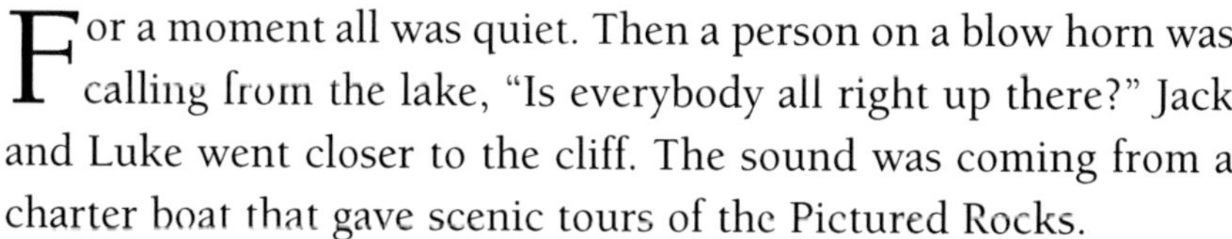

For a moment all was quiet. Then a person on a blow horn was calling from the lake, "Is everybody all right up there?" Jack and Luke went closer to the cliff. The sound was coming from a charter boat that gave scenic tours of the Pictured Rocks.

Jack cupped his hands around his mouth and yelled, "We're all right, but three men are injured and one is dead. Call the authorities and tell them where we are."

There were many people on the boat looking up at Luke and Jack, and then down toward the rocky shore. Jack and Luke also looked down to see the misshapen form of the once powerful man. His legs had obviously been broken during the fall as they were laying at strange angles. He was lying on his back, gazing upward with the terrified stare of one meeting death. His right arm was above him and moved back and forth in the water that came onto the rocks with each wave. Luke could see the black and blue wrist where Uncle Jack had held tight as the two men fought over the knife.

Jack gently grabbed Luke's shoulder and they moved back away from the cliff again. There was silence for a long time before Jack spoke. Luke gently petted Sam, who was content to just sit and enjoy Luke.

"I apologize to you, Luke," Jack began. "I could have disabled that man and made it so he couldn't get up and use that gun, but I wanted to punish him a little for what he said to us and especially what he said about you. He angered me and that anger cost a man his life. I'm sorry you had to see that."

Luke didn't know what to say, so for once he didn't say anything. He was just glad it was over and they were all okay, including Sam.

"Let's get our stuff and go see if we can find Buster. We'll have to talk to the authorities, and there will be an investigation. We may have to stick around a few days." Jack got up to leave. "My pistol must have come out of the holster when I ran through that brush a hundred yards back."

The walk back to the camp went quickly, it seemed, as Luke continued thinking about all that had happened. Jack found his pistol in the brush where he thought he lost it. He removed the clip and cleaned the sand off with an old blue handkerchief. Finally, satisfied with the cleanness of the pistol, he replaced it in the holster behind his back. Jack then told him about the men he had overtaken.

The camp was filthy, with the smell of dog feces so strong it made Luke almost gag. Several dogs were tied and began barking as they entered camp. Jack told Luke to stay with Sam and not go any further, as there would surely be another dog fight otherwise.

Jack didn't find Buster tied up outside so went into the fenced-in area between the two cabins. Soon he came out leading Buster, who didn't seem to be suffering any ill effects from his trip. Jack made a wide berth around the dogs so Buster would not mingle with them. As they came closer to Luke, Sam began to growl. Luke tried to stop him but Sam continued. Jack explained that these men were in the business of training fighting dogs and Sam had to fight to survive.

"He isn't going to make friends with any dog very easily," Jack said. "We'll just keep them apart and maybe they'll get used to each other."

Luke and Jack walked up the two-track toward the jeep. As they arrived at the gravel road, they heard sirens coming down the road to meet them. The sheriff, a short stocky man, got out of the first car and Jack began explaining what had brought Luke and him here and all the events of the day. The sheriff sent deputies to pick up the three men Jack had subdued. Jack spoke in lower tones about the death of the skinhead, so as not to cause Luke any more emotional trauma. Luke also heard the sheriff ask Jack where he lived and what he did for a living. Jack politely told him that he lived in the Washington, DC area and his job was classified, but he could give the sheriff a phone number that would put him in contact with people that would vouch for him.

Soon there were officials running all over the grounds. An animal control officer went back to the camp. An ambulance went down the two-track, possibly to try to bring back the body of the skinhead. Luke was content to watch all these things. He was happy to be with Sam, and he was thankful to be alive. Not much else seemed important.

Several deputies soon came out of the woods with the three men. The skinny little guy was still in a daze, with blood all over his face. The second man was holding his hand close to his side and blood also covered his face. Further away, two officers struggled to help the large man hobble toward the two-track. He couldn't let the one officer help prop him up because of his bad shoulder, so both officers had the big man's left arm over their backs, trying to balance him as he hobbled in the sand. Each time he moved, the two officers lost their footing and almost fell. It would have been humorous if the man wasn't in so much pain. The sheriff stopped talking and watched as the three men passed him on their way to the squad cars. As the big man hobbled by he looked at Jack, not with anger but with respect, but that expression was short lived because of his discomfort.

The sheriff continued looking at the men as they walked toward the waiting cars. Then he turned to Jack. "Are you sure there weren't more of you here?" he asked, half smiling but also not believing Jack could have caused so much trouble.

Luke then said, "You forgot to tell him about the dead attack dogs, Uncle Jack."

"Attack dogs!" the sheriff shouted. "Now come on, two of you caused all this chaos by yourselves! I don't believe it."

Jack tried to calm him down by going over the plan he and Luke had thought up and told the sheriff in stepwise fashion how everything unfolded.

The sheriff got up and walked over to Luke. "Let me see your bow," he said pointing to the tree Luke had propped it up against. "Who taught you to shoot so good?" the sheriff asked.

"I don't shoot that good, sir," Luke said. "I guess you learn to shoot straight if your life depends on it." The sheriff liked the humility and respect the young man showed.

Soon more people came carrying the dead dogs on canvas gurneys they had brought with them. The sheriff looked at Jack again as the dogs were carried away. He then just shook his head. "I don't know who you really are, or what you do, but you are one dangerous hombre. I don't think I want to get on your bad side." Jack smiled politely and sat patiently until all questions were answered.

"I want you to come into Munising and spend the next couple of days, until we sort through this mess. You're free to go," the sheriff said as he turned and started walking toward the camp.

Chapter 16

"Let's go, Luke," Jack said as he got up to leave, leading Buster. Luke had to keep his distance from Jack because Sam and Buster might fight. The ride back to the camper was somewhat cramped, as Luke had to keep Sam in the back and Buster sat in the front passenger seat of the jeep.

Luke was fondly stroking Sam on his back when he felt a little moisture. Looking at his hand he saw a small amount of blood. He knew Sam was probably injured but hadn't seen anything before. He gently parted the hair over the back of Sam's neck and found several bite wounds, punctures made by the skinhead's giant dog. Sam did not show pain but his skin began to quiver as Luke explored further. Luke even thought there was a depression over one area on Sam's neck that just didn't feel natural.

"I think Sam's hurt," Luke said to Jack as they pulled into the camp ground. "I should have looked him over sooner," Jack said as he got out of the jeep. "I'll leave Buster in the jeep for awhile. Bring Sam out into the sunlight and let's see what's going on."

By now Sam was stiffening up and had a little trouble jumping down out of the back end of the jeep, and he couldn't move his head very well. Jack gently parted the hair as Luke held Sam's head and reassured him. After examining the back of Sam's neck for many seconds, Jack turned to Luke and said, "He has several bite wounds and it feels like there's some muscle damage. We'd better pack up and get into Munising and get him treated. I hope Munising has a vet clinic."

Jack and Luke took a little time to clean up and change clothes before loading up all the stuff, hooking the jeep onto the truck, and then heading for Munising. Jack left Buster in the jeep so he wouldn't bother Sam, who Luke put in the front seat of the pickup truck with them. Sam rested some but Luke could tell he was in pain, especially if he tried to raise his head. Luke was mad at himself for not seeing the injuries before.

Within thirty minutes they were within the city limits of Munising. It was mid-afternoon and the tourists made the small town seem more busy than Luke had envisioned. Jack stopped at a gas station to ask directions to a veterinarian. Soon they were pulling into the parking lot of a clinic, which looked like a house that had been converted. Jack got out and looked at Buster, who seemed to be content in the jeep. He opened the windows a little more to make sure he had good ventilation.

"He should be all right since we parked in the shade. I'll come back and get him out after we get Sam looked at," Jack said as he came around to Luke's side of the truck to help get Sam out. By this time Sam was having trouble moving, and he groaned audibly as Jack and Luke lifted him out of the truck. Once on the ground he walked slowly with his head down and Luke and Jack directed him into the clinic.

Inside, a smiling receptionist in a colorful smock greeted the threesome. Jack explained the problem and the receptionist ushered them into a sunny exam room with a stainless steel table in the middle.

"Dr. Rollings will be with you in a few minutes. He's just finishing a surgery on a cat," she said as she left the room, closing the door.

Luke looked around the small room, thinking that although it looked like a house, it had the medicinal smells of a doctor's office. The room was very clean and everything was tidy. It looked like a good place to bring Sam. He wanted to pet Sam but was afraid that even his slight hand pressure might cause pain so he just talked softly to Sam and encouraged him. Jack just looked at Sam and then at Luke.

"He's going to be all right, Luke," Jack finally said, seeing the rising anxiety in Luke's face.

Just then the door opened and a rather tall, thin man with slightly graying hair and a white coat entered the room.

Chapter 16

"Hello," he said. "I'm Dr. Rollings, the receptionist told me you have a sick dog. How can I help you?"

Jack briefly explained about the dog fight and the wounds Luke had found, and the apparent discomfort that Sam was now experiencing, as the veterinarian listened intently, occasionally looking at Sam. Dr. Rollings knelt and looked into Sam's eyes, lifting the eyelids as he gently touched Sam.

"It sounds like you're a brave dog, Sam. Now we've got to fix you up so you can go back home," he said as he put a stethoscope to his ears and listened to Sam's heart and lungs. Satisfied, he gently palpated the abdomen and then all four limbs before coming back to the neck, which he examined for quite some time, even taking a pen light from his pocket to examine the bite wounds more thoroughly.

Finally finished, Dr. Rollings stood up and looked at Luke. "Sam's vital signs are good," he began, "and I don't feel he has any other injuries, but these bite wounds are fairly serious. Although they look like small puncture wounds, underneath there is extensive muscle damage. We need to put him on IVs, anesthetize him, and try to repair the torn muscle. We'll probably have to put some drainage tubes in there, and keep him on high doses of antibiotics for ten days or so. He should do well, but I can tell you more after I've seen the extent of the muscle damage."

Luke didn't know what to say, and Jack, sensing Luke's uneasiness, talked to the doctor. "Will he have to stay overnight?" Jack asked.

"Yes, and maybe staying a couple of days would be better. We can treat the wounds better and there would be less risk of infection, which is my most serious concern. We'll get started on him right away. We're not that busy right now. I'll call you when we are finished."

"Luke, do you have any questions?" Jack asked.

Luke shifted uneasily before asking, "How much will all this cost?"

Jack laughed. "Don't worry, Luke. I'll take care of it. Just do what you need to, Doctor."

Jack encouraged Luke to pet Sam and say good-bye, which Luke did reluctantly. "Do you need any help, Doctor?" Luke asked, obviously uneasy about leaving Sam after finally getting him back.

"No, thanks," Dr. Rollings said, smiling. "We have lots of help and he'll be just fine. Don't worry. I'll do my best to help him."

Turning to leave, Jack remembered Buster and asked if they could board him while Sam was at the clinic as they didn't have a place to keep him. Dr. Rollings assured him they had room for Buster, and Jack went out and brought Buster into the clinic. Jack and Luke both petted him and handed the leash to the ever-cheerful receptionist, who treated Buster like he was the only dog she'd seen that day. Buster wagged his tail and followed her back to the boarding facility.

Jack forgot about not having a phone and waited for the receptionist to return. "We're going to get a room at one of the motels and we'll call back and leave a number where Dr. Rollings can reach us after surgery. Then Jack and Luke went back to the truck.

"They seemed like real nice people, didn't they, Luke?" Jack asked as they got into the truck.

"Yeah, and Dr. Rollings seemed to like Sam, didn't he?" Luke replied.

"He did a thorough exam, and seems knowledgeable. I trust him." Jack started the truck and pulled out of the driveway. "I saw a motel at the edge of town that had a pool and sauna. That's just what we need to relax, don't you think?"

Luke, for the first time since this trip began, took time to realize he felt tired, stiff, dirty, and most of all, hungry. "That sounds good to me. I'm starved."

Jack laughed. "We haven't had much time to eat or relax, have we? Let's get a room, take a hot shower, and get a good dinner."

When they arrived at the motel they got a room on the second floor and took some of their things up to the room. Jack called the vet clinic to give the motel number while Luke took a shower.

The hot water felt good as it hit Luke on his face, head, neck, and shoulders. He hadn't felt this dirty and sore since the time last summer he stayed in the hay mow all day as his dad and brothers unloaded hay from the wagon into the elevator. Luke was glad his farm experience had helped train him for what he had gone through today. He had thought he was in good shape, but it was obvious he wasn't as fit as he thought. He wondered how Jack was able to move so fast, be so strong and fight like he did, all without even acting like he was even the least bit tired. Soon he was done showering and changed into clean clothes. He lay on one of the beds, stretched out flat on his back while Jack showered. He must have dozed off because the next thing he knew the phone was ringing and Jack was answering it, dressed in clean clothes, wearing a short-sleeved shirt. He had four small bandages on his left forearm where the dogs had bitten him.

"That's great news, Doctor," Jack concluded as he finished listening to what the veterinarian had to say. "We'll call you tomorrow morning and see how he's doing. Thanks for all your help." Hanging up, Jack told Luke that Sam was resting well. He had quite a bit of muscle damage but should heal nicely.

"That's a relief," Luke said as he propped himself up on his elbows.

As Luke continued to lie on the bed, Jack dialed another number and waited patiently for someone to answer. "Hi, Nancy. It's Uncle Jack. Is your mom there?" he asked and waited a second. "Hi, Martha. We're fine. My cell phone won't work way up here in the Upper Peninsula. We're in Munising, and we got both dogs back. Everything didn't go as we planned, and we'll have to stay over and talk to the sheriff and we also have to wait for Sam to be discharged from the vet's. I'll let you talk to Luke." Jack handed the phone receiver to Luke, who was now sitting on the side of the bed.

"Hi, Mom," Luke tried to say in his most enthusiastic voice.

"You sound tired, Luke. Was there any trouble? Are you sure you're all right?"

"Yes, Mom, I'm fine," Luke answered. "I just woke up from a short nap. I'm glad Uncle Jack remembered to call as it completely slipped my mind, I was so concerned about Sam. Is every one okay at home?"

"We're all fine. When are you coming home?"

"Probably the day after tomorrow, because Sam may have to stay at the vet's a day or two. I'd better get ready to go eat supper," Luke concluded. "Uncle Jack and I are really hungry!"

"Okay, Luke, bye! I love you."

"I love you too, Mom," Luke said as he hung up the phone.

"Let's go eat!" Jack said, realizing Luke was a little embarrassed about telling his mom he loved her.

As they drove to a restaurant in downtown Munising, Luke told Jack he was so relieved about Sam he thought he might like to be a veterinarian.

"It's a fine profession, and you do seem to have a way with animals. How are your grades in school?" Jack asked.

"They're pretty good, and I'm taking college prep classes, but I never really thought much about what I wanted to do after high school. I never really thought hard about it, you know what I mean?" Luke said, surprised at his own seriousness about his future.

"I think it takes at least six years of college to graduate, but anything worthwhile is not easy," Jack said as they pulled into the parking lot of the restaurant.

Chapter 16

Luke and Jack ordered steak, baked potato, and garden salad. Before they ate, Jack bowed his head to pray. Luke was a little embarrassed, but also bowed his head slightly and closed his eyes as Jack began to pray out loud. "Heavenly Father," Jack began. "Thank you for our safety today, and thank you for helping us get Buster and Sam back. Please help Sam to heal quickly. I'm sorry for losing my temper today. It cost a man his life. Thank you for your love for us, and thank you for this food. Amen."

Luke looked up just in time to see the waitress bringing their food. Luke had never tasted a better steak, he thought, as they finished their meal. After the meal Luke felt more tired than he ever felt in his life, so they went back to the motel and went to bed. Luke barely remembered getting undressed.

Chapter 17

When Luke woke up it was already daylight. Jack was out of the room but soon returned. He had gone for his morning run.

"I hope you're not forming any bad habits by sleeping so late," he teased. "It's almost six-thirty A.M. and you're still in bed."

Luke propped himself up on his elbows, his favorite position, and looked at Jack, not really knowing what to say. He wasn't used to sleeping in and he felt guilty, reminding himself that his dad and brothers had already been up for an hour and were doing his chores.

"I'm going to take a shower," Jack said as he started taking off his sweatshirt. His forearm was a little more bruised than it had appeared yesterday, but he didn't seem to favor it. "Then we'd better get some breakfast and go talk to the sheriff. You'll have to tell him what you saw and he'll ask me a bunch of questions too. When that's finished, let's go for a boat ride and tour Pictured Rocks. It's cloudy and a little rainy but it's supposed to clear up this afternoon. I also should talk to Dr. Rollings about taking that tracking device out of Buster's scruff so we won't have to stop on our way back home."

Jack took a quick shower as Luke got dressed. Soon they were on their way to breakfast. Luke was still hungry and ordered bacon, eggs, and hot cakes. Jack didn't seem as hungry and ate oatmeal and wheat toast. Jack tried to keep the conversation light, knowing Luke would have to relive the events of yesterday all over again at the sheriff's office.

After their meal, the two went back to the motel. Jack made a few phone calls, and Luke stepped outside so as not to overhear his conversation, as Jack acted a little uneasy when he said he had to call into work and tell them what was going on. At nine-thirty, Jack called the vet clinic to see how Sam was and to ask the veterinarian to remove the tracking device from Buster. Satisfied with his answer, Jack thanked the doctor again and hung up.

"Sam's doing fine," Jack told Luke. "We can pick him up about this time tomorrow. There's some aftercare that Dr. Rollings will demonstrate tomorrow, but Sam's going to be as good as new. We'd better get to the sheriff's office before he comes looking for us," Jack said, smiling.

The sheriff's office seemed quiet to Luke, who was expecting the busy atmosphere he saw on television cop shows. They had to wait briefly but were then escorted into the sheriff's office. He was on the phone so Jack and Luke sat down across from him and waited. The sheriff's desk did not appear cluttered, in fact it was quite neat. Luke thought the sheriff looked quite different with his hat off than when he'd seen him yesterday, but the voice was the same, reminding him of Jimmy Stewart, his mom's favorite actor.

Finishing the phone conversation, the sheriff shifted his attention to Jack and Luke. There was silence as the sheriff looked from Jack to Luke and then back to Jack again. "It's hard to believe the two of you could cause such a disturbance. We talked to the three men, who are still in the hospital, by the way. Your story pretty much checks out, but I've got a few questions for each of you." The sheriff picked up the phone and issued an order. Soon a deputy came into the room, a young, athletic, light-haired man with a short hair cut, not quite a buzz cut, but a crew cut, Al would have called it.

"Luke, you go with officer Flynn. He'll ask you some questions, and your uncle and I will stay here and do the same, okay?" the sheriff said.

"Sure," was all Luke said, rising from the chair, looking at Jack for assurance.

Jack winked and smiled. "Just tell the truth, son, and everything will be fine," he told Luke, sensing that Luke was a little uneasy.

The deputy led Luke down the hall to a small room. "Do you want something to drink before we get started?" the deputy asked.

"Just a glass of water," Luke said, as he could feel his throat getting dry. Luke sat in one of the two chairs in the room. Between the two chairs was a small wooden table with a yellow legal pad. The deputy returned with a large paper cup filled with water, and Luke took a swallow. The water was cold and tasted good. The deputy sat down and tried to put Luke at ease, asking where he lived and what grade he was in, things Luke could easily answer. Soon Luke was explaining the sequence of events that had brought him to this area. He explained how Jack had merely intended to get enough information about the dog thieves to come to the sheriff but Jack's cell phone failed and the quick shift in wind direction changed everything.

Luke then told the officer how he had to shoot the first dog for fear of his life. Then he told about Jack fighting the other two dogs, and then how Jack led the other three men away from him while he got into a safer location, only to be found by his own dog,

Sam. Then he talked about the skinhead finding him, and the fight Sam had had with the huge mastiff-type dog.

"How is your dog?" the officer interrupted. "I heard you had to take him to Dr. Rollings."

"He's going to be fine, but he's got to stay at the vet's one more day," Luke said.

"Now, tell me in detail about what happened next and try not to leave anything out, because a man lost his life yesterday and this is important, son," the officer said, looking quite serious.

Luke took another drink of the cool water that tasted a lot like the water back home. Then he told the officer everything he could remember, finishing with Sam charging the skinhead and pushing him off the cliff, and Uncle Jack grabbing Sam's leg so he didn't fall with the skinhead.

The officer was writing as Luke was talking, sometimes briefly looking up at Luke, encouraging him to continue.

"I can't think of anything else," Luke said finally. The officer kept writing for a minute as Luke sat there.

"What does your uncle do for a living?" the officer finally asked.

Luke explained that he didn't know and his dad had told him not to ask.

"Whatever he does," the officer said, "he must be a martial arts specialist, or a mean street fighter, or both. That's the only part I have trouble believing, Luke. It doesn't seem possible that one man could do all this to four men and not be hurt himself."

Luke didn't know what to say, but assured the officer that he was telling the truth. "Oh, I believe you son," the officer said. "The men in the hospital say the same thing. One guy doesn't remember anything, but the other two said your uncle moved so fast they couldn't hardly do anything to defend themselves."

"He was a state champion wrestler in high school," Luke said, thinking that might explain some of Jack's abilities.

The officer laughed, wrote that in his notes, and then kept chuckling as he thought about what Luke had said. Luke, realizing how he sounded, was embarrassed and grabbed the cup of water, taking another drink.

"I think we're done here," officer Flynn said. "Let's go back and see if the sheriff is finished taking your uncle's statement. They walked back down the hall to the sheriff's office, where Jack and the sheriff were engaged in normal conversation. The sheriff pointed to the chair where Luke had sat previously and then the sheriff and deputy left the office to compare notes.

Jack looked at Luke. "Are you doing okay?"

Luke was relieved that most of the questioning was over and it probably showed on his face, as he didn't even bother answering.

It wasn't long until the sheriff came back into the room. "It looks like your story checks out," the sheriff told Luke. "You're both free to go. I've got your phone numbers and addresses as you may have to testify at some time. That man, Jim Dorsey, had a rap sheet longer than my arm. He was wanted in three states for various crimes, the worst being kidnapping, suspected murder, and child pornography. I really think dog fighting was just his hobby. He was a very dangerous man and I'm glad to have him off the streets."

Luke couldn't help but notice that the sheriff treated Jack differently than he had yesterday, showing more respect and admiration. He overheard the sheriff tell Jack to stop into the office if he was ever in the area again. The sheriff then shook hands with Jack and Luke and they left.

Chapter 18

The clouds were beginning to lift as Luke and Jack headed for the pickup. The sun even showed itself briefly between passing clouds. Luke thought the clouds moved much faster up here than at home, and it was entertaining just watching the clouds pass through the sky.

"Let's go see when the next boat leaves for Pictured Rocks," Jack said, interrupting Luke's thoughts.

"Yeah," Luke said. "I've never gone out in a boat that big."

"Well, it's not a large ship, but it's big enough to take us out on Lake Superior in comfort. You'll be impressed with the rock formations and the sheer beauty of the place, especially if the sun is shining on the rocks this afternoon."

It was a short drive down to the tour boat office and gift shop. They parked the truck and went into the gift shop to see the schedule. "We'll have to buy some things for your family while we're here," Jack said as he looked over some of the merchandise. He got in line and bought two boat tickets. Luke was looking at pictures of light houses when Jack returned to tell him the boat would be loading in a few minutes.

"I didn't know Lake Superior was so big," Luke exclaimed, as he looked at a big map of the lake.

"I heard there's enough water in Lake Superior to cover the whole U.S. in five feet of water," Jack said as they left the store and walked to the dock. Soon they were allowed to board the boat, and Luke noted how sturdy the boat felt, much different than the row boat he had fished from when he visited his Uncle Bob. He could feel the waves underneath, and the gentle rocking of the boat seemed soothing after the stress of answering questions all morning.

Within minutes they were on their way, the diesel motor of the boat humming much like the tractor back home. There were not many people on the boat, which the captain said was probably due to the rainy morning and the unexpected appearance of the sun. The boat chugged out of the bay, past Grand Island, and into the open water of the big lake. Luke couldn't get enough of the blue water, highlighted by the bright sunshine and the feeling of exhilaration that the cool wind blowing off the lake brought to his tanned face. He looked at Jack, who also seemed to sense what Luke was feeling. It was as though they had left their concerns back on land and were moving away from them.

The boat traveled northeast at a steady pace and soon the beginning of the rock formations came into view, whitish columns rising out of the bright blue water. The beauty of this place was really beyond description, and Luke and Jack tried to take it all in, etching it into their memories. Jack reached into his jacket pocket and pulled out a disposable camera he had bought at the gift shop. He took a few pictures when the lighting was just right and the boat lined up with the shore at the proper angle.

"We'll get pictures so you can show your family where you came on your vacation," Jack said as he continued to try to take the perfect picture. "Over the years I've visited a lot of places in this world, and I still think this is the most beautiful."

Chapter 18

Luke, being untraveled, took Jack's word for it, as it seemed so majestic, and somehow peaceful, even though the obvious unbridled power of the lake made one feel small and insignificant.

As the boat continued in its easterly path along the shoreline Luke recognized the cliff that the skinhead had fallen from, somewhere close to Chapel Rock, the tour guide said. Luke looked at the cliffs, with trees sticking up at various angles along their tops, and the bed of rock beneath, with several huge boulders jutting out from the water's surface, waves forever pounding against them, first exposing more rock and then suddenly hiding it in an oncoming swell. The place looked so peaceful and serene, but had been the scene of death just one day before.

Jack looked at Luke to see how he responded to the memories of yesterday. "Luke," Jack said, "I brought you out here to see the beauty of this place, and to share it with you, but I also brought you here to help you understand more about what happened yesterday so you will be able to cope with it in the future. I want to apologize for putting you in harm's way. I never intended for you to be in danger, and I was relying on the wind not changing direction, which is in reality a foolish assumption, especially along this lake. As a result of my foolishness you had to witness some violence that would repulse most people. I wanted to shelter you from that and I failed, but the worst part is, I lost my temper when the skinhead said he was going to harm you after he got rid of me.

"That made me lose my focus, and gave him an opportunity to draw his gun, which almost led to all our deaths. That man's death was unnecessary, as I normally would have disabled him and frisked him to make sure he had no more weapons. We're just lucky Sam was there to attack him or we'd be dead today. That frightens me, but it saddens me greatly that this man died without any hope." Luke remembered the look of terror on the man's face as he had cautiously peered at him from the top of the cliff. He would never forget the look of hatred he had while fighting Jack and then that look of terror, with his eyes fixed in that gaze that comes when one passes from life to death.

Luke was a little confused. His uncle said he was mad at the skinhead for what he did and what he planned to do, but was saddened at his death, which seemed like a contradiction. Luke remained quiet for several minutes as the boat continued on its eastward path along the rugged shoreline.

"How can you feel sorry for that man?" Luke finally asked. "He was going to kill us." Luke didn't like the idea of the skinhead dying, but preferred that to the alternative.

"I guess it goes back to my personal beliefs," Jack started to explain. "Let me tell you what I believe and maybe it will make more sense. When I was about your age, I was overwhelmed with the decisions I had to make about college, career, girls, and all the other things teenagers face. I felt that my life didn't have a purpose, that I wasn't focused on anything. I was like this boat with the engine shut off. I'd just drift along with the waves until I hit the shore, having no control.

"It was about this time that I felt God encouraging me to come to Him. I started reading in the New Testament, especially the books of Mark and John, and realized God loved me and had a plan for my life. I recognized that I could not really know God because I was imperfect, as all humans are, born with a sinful nature. God already knew this, and sent His Son, Jesus, to pay the penalty for sin for us, so that we can have a personal relationship with God. I accepted what Jesus did for me, and received Him as my Savior.

"That single act changed my life forever. From then on, my focus was on God and what He wanted me to do and He has helped me make all of life's decisions. Some people say I have 'religion,' but it's not religion; it's a relationship with the God that made heaven and earth. And I know He loves me, and wants to be a big part of my life. That's why it saddened me to see that man die, because I know that without that personal relationship with God, he was bound for eternity without God. I think that is why he had such a look of terror on his face, not because of the fall."

Jack looked at Luke and Luke looked into Jack's eyes, seeing they were a little moist with emotion. Luke could tell that Jack loved him and it made Luke feel needed, appreciated, and important.

"I know I've been struggling with decisions about my future, too," Luke finally said, trying hard to choose the right words. "I also feel like my life is not controlled by me, and I merely react to what happens from one day to the next. I've gone to church most of my life, but didn't really see the need to have a personal relationship with God, but I know that He's been talking to me the last few days, showing me that He cares for me. I need Him in my life, and I feel He is drawing me to Him. Thanks, Uncle Jack, for helping me understand."

Luke bowed his head and talked to God, confessing the sin in his life, and receiving Christ into his heart. A deep sense of relief and satisfaction overwhelmed Luke, and he opened his eyes and saw Jack fondly looking at him.

"I did it," was all Luke said.

Jack reached over and hugged Luke. Luke could feel Jack's arm muscles tighten and was again surprised at the strength he possessed, although he wasn't hurt; he just had the feeling he was engulfed by someone much stronger than himself, much like a baby in the arms of a loving parent.

By now the boat was turning around to begin its trip back to Munising.

"Now your life is like this boat," Jack illustrated. "This boat is steered by the pilot, and your life is now steered by God. You just have to stay in a close relationship with Him, so you are aware of what He wants you to do. Remember, He wants what's best for you and you have to trust Him completely. He'll help you make these tough decisions. You just need to read your Bible, because He talks to you through His Word, and you need to talk to Him, by praying. It's important to stay in this close relationship at all times so you can hear what He's telling you. This is how I live my life, and my life has meaning because I'm doing what he has planned for my life. It's like shooting your bow. If you don't concentrate on a single spot, you won't be able to hit the mark."

It all made sense to Luke and he saw more clearly than he had ever seen before. He felt his life did have a purpose, and that he had someone to guide him through every aspect of his life and it felt good. But more important, it felt right and there was a peace in his heart he had never had before.

As he looked up at the rocks he saw a bald eagle soaring effortlessly overhead. Luke had never seen an eagle before and he eagerly nudged Jack and pointed upward. Before them was the perfect picture and Jack took a photo. The blue sky, with hints of white high clouds, the bright sun, the rugged rocks and cliffs, and the incessant beating of the waves on the shoreline—that was beautiful enough, but adding that majestic bald eagle, soaring over the cliffs, the wind causing his feathers to ruffle slightly as he flew and the wildness that he personified, created an indelible impression on Luke's and Jack's minds.

The trip back to Munising seemed to take longer than the trip out to the rocks. A storm blew in from Lake Superior and in seconds it was raining and the wind was blowing large waves that made the boat roll back and forth as it chugged back to the bay. Luke was surprised at the awesome power of the lake, and how quickly the storm blew in upon them. He thought of the many ships that had gone down in the harsh storms of November, and knew this small storm was nothing like that, but he was intrigued by the wildness of this lake that could not be tamed by humans.

Once back at the dock, Jack and Luke went into the gift shop and Jack bought some things for Luke's brothers, sisters, and mom.

Chapter 18

Luke saw a pay phone and told Jack he wanted to make a phone call. Jack gave a phone card to him so he wouldn't have to keep adding money while talking. Luke thanked him, assuring Jack he would pay him back when they got home.

"I'll be looking around in the gift shop. Come get me when you finish," Jack said after giving instructions on how to use the card.

Luke had memorized Sue's number and was glad that she answered the phone.

"Luke?" she said, surprised.

"Hi, I'm up in the U.P.," Luke began. "I've been doing a lot of thinking up here and I want you to know I would like to take you out when I get back home, maybe even this Saturday, if that's okay." There was brief silence.

"Luke, you sound different. Are you okay?" she asked, somewhat concerned. "Let me ask my mom if I can go out. I'll be right back." There was a long silence that gave Luke time to observe the last of the storm blow off the lake. As the clouds rolled to the south the sun made another appearance, but the wind off the lake remained cool.

"Luke," Sue said, returning to the phone, "I can go." Luke thought she sounded excited about going out with him.

"Good, I'll call you when I get back home and talk to my folks."

"Are you having a good time up there?" Sue asked.

"Yes," Luke replied, wishing he had said something more witty or profound. Then he added, "My uncle and I went on a boat tour of Pictured Rocks today." He wanted to tell her about finding his dog and the adventure that he had, but didn't know how to begin, and thought it might sound too gross.

"Well, I'd better go," Luke said.

"I'm glad you called, Luke," Sue said.

As Luke hung up he felt good knowing Sue cared for him. That was important to him and he knew he wanted to be with her and get to know her better.

Luke went into the store and found Jack, who was looking at pictures of the various light houses along the shore of Lake Superior. As they got into the truck to go back to the motel Luke turned to Jack and asked, "Don't you ever get lonely for a girlfriend?" The way he said it didn't come out right, and Luke felt sorry he even brought it up, but Jack just laughed it off, making Luke feel better, because he didn't want to do anything to make his uncle think badly of him.

"I've dated several women," Jack began, "and even have gotten serious a time or two, but I just don't think it would be fair to a woman to ask her to put up with all the things I have to do in my line of work. I'm out of the country a lot, and sometimes I'm in situations that would make a woman who cared about me very uneasy, so I've just decided not to get serious about a relationship until I get into a different line of work. Your dad told me you had a date recently. Are you getting serious about this girl?"

Luke's face felt suddenly warm, and he knew he was blushing. "No . . . I'm not serious. Well . . ." he stammered, before Jack interrupted.

"If I were you, I would get to know this girl well, but don't get too serious at your age," Jack advised. "You have your whole life in front of you, and you have a lot of decisions to make. Don't rush into anything and make sure you know that you will be making some decisions that will affect the rest of your life. Remember, you now have a Pilot to guide your ship, too, so make sure you ask Him to help you with your decisions."

"Yeah, I know." Luke said. "I still feel overwhelmed when I think about all the things I have to decide in the next couple of years, but I don't have to do it alone."

"No, you don't," Jack said, "and you've got your mom and dad to help, and you can call me if you want my advice, too. I know you have a lot of decisions but usually you don't have to make more than one decision at a time, so don't get overwhelmed, and take time to enjoy each day as a gift from God."

Chapter 19

The next morning Luke helped Jack hook up the jeep to the truck. Then they had a good breakfast before going to pick up Sam and Buster. Sam was happy to see Luke and wagged his tail as hard as he could to show him just how glad he really was. Dr. Rollings gave Luke a small bottle of Betadine Solution and carefully showed him how to clean around the drain tubes before infusing two cc's directly into the hole in the skin where the one drain tube came out. He then showed him how to remove the drain tubes in three days, and then the sutures in another week. Then he gave Luke a ten-day supply of antibiotic tablets.

"Do you have any questions?" Dr. Rollings asked Luke when he had finished. Luke had Dr. Rollings show him again how to infuse the medicine into the wound, and then he felt confident he could do everything properly.

"Did I mention Luke is thinking about being a veterinarian?" Jack said to Dr. Rollings.

"No, I didn't know. It's a good profession son, and very rewarding, but it also takes a lot of studying and hard work. Your farm background will help you, and I know you're accustomed to hard work already, so I would say you could do it if you made up your mind to be a veterinarian. Maybe you should spend time at your local veterinarian's office and go with him on some farm calls. That'll give you a good idea about what the life of a veterinarian is like," Dr. Rollings said.

"Thanks, Doctor," Luke said, "and thanks for fixing Sam. He feels a lot better, I can tell," he said as he gently petted Sam, who was leaning against his left leg, soaking up all the attention.

Sam didn't even growl when the technician brought Buster into the lobby, although they looked at each other for a long time. Dr. Rollings gave Jack a small box, explaining that the monitor was cleaned up and still in good working order. He then told Luke that Buster's sutures could come out on the same day that Sam's were to be removed, to keep it simple.

"Thanks again, Dr. Rollings," Jack said as they left the building.

Once they got to the truck, Jack told Luke to sit in the back seat with Sam and Buster could sit in the front seat, so the two dogs wouldn't get close enough to fight. "In time, they'll do fine together, but Sam has been through a lot, and was in the process of being trained to kill other dogs, so you'll have to watch him around other pets for quite some time," Jack explained as they loaded the dogs.

"If we start right now, we'll be home in ten hours," Jack told Luke as they left town, heading east on M-28. Luke sat quietly in the back seat with one hand resting on Sam, who was lying on the seat beside him, his warm body pressing against Luke's side, showing Luke he didn't want to ever be separated again.

"Someday, I'm going to live up here," Luke said, breaking the silence after they had traveled several miles.

"You like it up here, I take it," Jack answered.

"It's beautiful, and not crowded with people, and there's a feeling that this is a place that hasn't been tamed. There are so many wild places, and I'd like to see more of them and explore the rivers and woods." Luke couldn't put into words exactly how he felt, but he knew he wanted to spend more time here in "God's country," as Dr. Rollings put it.

Luke moved forward in the seat and started talking to Jack, who had his right hand on Buster, who was sprawled out on the passenger seat, sleeping peacefully.

"Thanks for taking time to come up here and get Sam," he began, trying not to get too emotional. "I know I'd never have gotten him back without you, and I'm glad you grabbed his leg as he jumped off that cliff. You almost fell off yourself, trying to save him. And thanks for all the money you've spent on me for meals, motel, and that phone call, too."

Jack smiled. "It's been fun getting to know you, Luke, and I've enjoyed this trip and the time spent with you. I've realized through this what I'm missing in my own life, and that is family. My work has become such a big part of my life that I haven't been able to focus on anything else, and that's going to change. Who knows, maybe I'll move back to Michigan sometime soon."

After thanking Jack and listening to what he said, Luke leaned back in his seat, relaxed and looked out his window at the Lake Michigan shoreline along U.S. 2. It was a calm, sunny day and there were no waves to be seen. Luke felt as calm inside as the surface of the lake. He had got Sam back, he had a good relationship with his uncle, and he had a personal relationship with the God who made this beautiful country. He felt blessed as he looked over at Sam, who was sleeping. Luke methodically stroked Sam's side telling Sam he was there, and he wasn't going to let anything happen to him again.

"Oh, I forgot something," Jack said as he leaned over and opened the glove box. "This is for you," he said, handing a small flat box to Luke. Luke opened the box and saw a Bible with a dark blue leather cover.

"Gee, thanks, Uncle Jack," Luke said. "You—"

Jack interrupted. "Look inside the cover."

On the inner cover was a picture Jack had taken of the eagle. The picture had a clear plastic cover and was attached to the inner cover. Under the picture, Uncle Jack had written these words:

> *But they that wait upon the Lord shall renew their strength; they shall mount up with wings like eagles; they shall run and not be weary; and they shall walk, and not faint.*
>
> *Isaiah 40:31*

Tears welled up in Luke's eyes as he looked at the verse, then at the picture, thinking of all that the picture of this eagle represented in his life. For a long moment he couldn't speak. Then, in a soft voice, he said, "Thank you so much. I love you, Uncle Jack."

Jack turned his head around to face his nephew. There were tears in his eyes too. "I love you, as much as if you were my own son," Jack said, reaching back and pressing Luke's knee with his right hand.

Far above, out of view of the weary travelers, an eagle looked down on the tiny, green truck as it lazily glided with the wind currents, content as he felt the warmth of the sun, and the cool breeze off the lake flowing through the feathers of his wings.

THE END

To order additional copies of

Have your credit card ready and call:

1-877-421-READ (7323)

or please visit our web site at
www.pleasantword.com

Also available at: www.amazon.com

CPSIA information can be obtained at www.ICGtesting.com
Printed in the USA
238414LV00002BA/165/A

9 781579 215613